sacred hearts

sacred hearts

a novel

GREG BOYD

davis / hi jinx press / 1996

acknowledgements

The author would like to thank Marie-José Fortis and Robert Peters, who read and commented on this novel in manuscript.

Printed in the United States of America.
ISBN 1-57650-049-7
Library of Congress Catalogue Number 96-76622

Hi Jinx Press
P. O. Box 1814
Davis, CA 95616

for donna

Mary, Mary
Quite contrary
How does your garden grow?
With Silver Bells and Cockleshells
And pretty maids all in a row.

— Nursery Rhyme

Blessed art thou among women
And blessed be the fruit of thy womb . . .

— Hail Mary

All things rising, all things sizing
Mary sees, sympathizing
    With that world of good,
    Nature's motherhood.

— Gerard Manley Hopkins,
"The May Magnificat"

There was a fine gal named Mary,
Of whom all the gents were wary.
    When her legs opened wide,
    She had buried inside,
More secrets than she could carry.

— Anonymous

Sacred hearts

My shift had ended and I was driving home under a full moon when I saw angels leap from a freeway overpass. Two of them, dressed in white and holding hands, were standing atop the railing. Though I was tired from being on my feet from three till eleven, I know what I saw. Just before my car reached them, they dropped together like they were jumping into a swimming pool. They must have been moving above me as my car disappeared beneath the bridge, though I didn't see them hit the pavement. I checked the rear view mirror, but saw only the glare of headlights on the road behind me.

It happened on a desolate stretch of highway surrounded by cotton fields. There was no place to stop and call for help, so I turned off at the first exit and drove down the service road back toward the bridge. When I got to the overpass there was nothing to see. Maybe someone had already taken them to the hospital, though I hadn't heard a siren. I parked my car and walked onto the bridge. Gripping the metal railing, I looked down at the blackness below, then stared a moment at the lights of the oncoming cars. When I got home, I was still shaking. I fixed myself a cup of tea and went to bed.

The next day I watched the television news and searched the newspaper headlines, but I couldn't find any mention of the accident. After I'd had my coffee, I got into my car and retraced my route, approaching the bridge several times from both directions. I was absolutely certain of what I'd seen. Finally I called the police, but they didn't have any information either. Instead, I got the feeling the person I was talking to thought I was crazy. I hung up when he asked for my name.

At the time I imagined the jumpers were unhappy lovers. I thought they might have made a suicide pact. With the divorce rate so high and just about everyone these days wishing for a more romantic love life, anything seemed possible—frustrated Romeo and Juliet high school kids, for example. But try as I might I couldn't figure how they'd disappeared behind me. Now I know better. They were angels, just as Sheila said.

Sheila was one of the girls I used to work with. Though she was older than me and quiet, we got along well. She wasn't bitchy and temperamental like the other waitresses, always stomping off mad to the kitchen to smoke cigarettes and complain about the management and the customers.

I'm not mean like that either, though I never could manage to smile the way Sheila did when a customer insisted on blaming me for his troubles. Whenever someone changed an order or complained about the food I'd turn it into a joke, make him laugh if I could. The truckers liked me. They said I was feisty. What they really meant, though, is I've got just what they like—which those little pink dresses we had to wear did little to hide—so they'd put up with my mouth. So even the complaints about poor service when we were understaffed and busy didn't get beyond me, except once or twice when some guy would come in with his wife or girlfriend who had it in for me.

I remember this one old broad—face creased like a road map—asked me for clean silverware must have been three different times. I kept bringing her sets straight from the service bin and already wrapped in napkins. Each time she'd call me back and point out some tiny spot. Finally, I took the fork from her, held it up to the light, brought it to my lips and spit on it. Then I wiped it on my apron and handed it back to her. "That should take care of it," I said. I was so mad I even winked at her husband. Of course she called the manager and tried her best to get me fired. He stood there with his hands in his pockets and told them he was sorry and they didn't have to pay for their meal. After they'd gone, the whole staff laughed about it.

Aside from the occasional cry-baby or chronic complainer, I always got good tips, especially from the truckers. Let's just say I knew how to humor them.

More to the point, I know what men like. And I'm not ashamed to admit that I appreciate the attention they pay me. In the restaurant eyes used to peek at me over the menu. Sometimes the truckers would try to embarrass me, make me blush and laugh. I remember one guy telling me, "Baby, your legs are so fine even them orthopedic shoes can't ruin them." I knew they loved seeing me fussed up, so I'd make a good show of it, maybe stand with my hands on my hips and shake my head or stamp my foot. Then they'd laugh.

Ever since my divorce three years earlier, I'd been having a pretty good time with men. As I used to tell Sheila: If it wasn't okay to eat, it wouldn't be on the menu. And as long as it's on your plate, you might as well put your face in it. So what if I wasn't much interested in getting myself a new husband? Is that all there is to life? Anyway, Sheila used to say I had a talent for picking up strays, though she didn't mean it in a nasty way.

Sheila wasn't anything like me in that sense. You'd never catch her wisecracking with the truckers. She was both a loner and a gentle soul. Somehow people can sense that kind of dignity and most of them respect it, too. I never once saw a man, not even the raunchiest, most wild-eyed, hopped-up cross-country hauler, treat Sheila with anything but politeness. It's as if she knew instinctively how to keep her distance from the men. Not that she couldn't attract them, with her round face and shy little smile. I'd seen how they tugged the brims of their hats and followed her with their eyes. But she never made any effort to fix herself up, not even a little lipstick or rouge, and she didn't even seem capable of flirting. Still, different as we were, Sheila and I got to be good friends.

Sometimes, when we were both off shift the same day, we visited or went shopping together. She'd follow me around while I tried on a pair of pumps and tested new perfumes on my wrist. Sometimes she bought soap or bubble bath. I remember how we'd sit at her kitchen table beneath the framed unicorn poster in the afternoon light and drink wine together. I can see her wearing sweat pants and fuzzy pink slippers. Everything she said seemed funny.

Another thing: I could tell her whatever I felt without her making me feel cheap. The other waitresses loved to talk behind my back. Once I overheard them gossiping about me and one of the new diesel mechanics. One of them even called me a tramp. I don't know why, but it hurt my feelings. I was crying out back by myself when Sheila put her hand on my shoulder. "They're just jealous, Mary," she said. Somehow she always knew the right thing to say.

Of course Sheila's not her real name. It's Mary, same as mine. But I was working at Toppers first and it was too confusing for the cooks and everyone else to have more than one Mary waitressing, so the night manager gave her a name tag he found that had belonged to a waitress who'd gotten married and quit a couple of years before. Pretty soon nobody at work would have thought of calling her anything but Sheila. And even though I called her that, too, I always remembered she was really Mary.

A guy I once dated told me all women are Mary, one way or another. He laughed when he said that and his lip curled like a dog's. It was a stupid thing to say and I suppose he meant that I was different from Sheila. I couldn't look at him after that without finding something cruel, so about a week later I made excuses and said I didn't want to see him again.

When I told Sheila about the jumpers she didn't smile. We were washing our hands with milky liquid soap in the ladies room, and the whole time I talked she stared straight into my eyes. I started speaking faster and faster and when I finally finished, she didn't say anything for a long time. Then she touched my arm. Her hand was still wet. "Let's get together after work," she whispered, "there's something I need to tell you." Then, without bothering to dry her hands or turn off the water in the sink, she turned and hurried toward her station.

After we'd both clocked out that night, Sheila and I sat together in my car in the parking lot. We'd no sooner locked the doors than Sheila told me she was quitting work the next day. She said it in a voice so distant it gave me goose bumps. My first thought was to talk her out of it, but she held up her hand like she wasn't finished, so I let her go on. That's when she told me about the message Jesus had sent her.

It seems the same night I'd seen the falling angels Sheila had walked home from work and turned on her television. Her apartment was not far from the grease pit we called work, so she must have been watching her program about the same time I had my vision. That's what she always called it. A vision. Anyway, there was a talk show on with a bunch of guys who claimed to be the holy flesh and spirit of Jesus Christ.

Of course that whole idea seems far-fetched, even ridiculous, at first. The point of this show, I'd guess, was that these characters weren't just a collection of lunatics, because all of them had people—disciples, I suppose you'd call them—who followed them around and believed everything they said was true. The best-known guest wasn't even a real Christian. He was an Indian— from India, I mean—and in his country lots of people thought he was a holy man. He claimed he'd lived other lives in the past and in all of them he was a prophet sacred to some tribe or religion. In one of those lives he was Jesus. Now he said he was doing it over, like déja-vu, I guess.

Some of the other guests made even less sense, especially the fat guy with the crew cut and the tight blue suit I saw on the video later who kept pointing at the others and saying that all Hindu sinners who didn't acknowledge his ministry would burn in hell like twigs in a wood stove. His face resembled steak tartare when he ranted and showed pictures of people handling rattlesnakes at his church. "Satan has no power in the presence of the Lord," he insisted.

Anyway, what she was getting at, Sheila said—and this is the really strange part—was that while watching these six men she got the feeling one of them was trying to communicate with her right through the television. "He was calling out to me and to me alone. He had something important and personal to tell me, but I couldn't quite understand," Sheila said. "It was like a bad phone connection. Too much static." Listening to her I thought for a minute I was going to laugh out loud right in her face, but as soon as my mouth started moving in that direction I remembered those two people jumping from the bridge and the laugh melted right back into the walls of my stomach.

I'd never seen Sheila so worked up. It wasn't like her to get excited. In fact, to my knowledge nothing ever bothered her—not nasty customers, nor one-day sales, nor even hormones boiling over on bad days. She'd always been quiet, resigned, and good-natured. But now I saw her hands flying around like bats in the neon-light. Her voice sounded deep, and at one point she started breathing so fast I thought she might collapse. Though it worried me to see her gasping for air one minute, a big smile spread across her face and tears running down her cheeks the next, I felt a spark there, too. The inside of the car seemed to be filling up with electricity, and I slowly began to tingle, almost the same as when a man's been loving me up a long time, kissing and running his hands along the inside of my thighs, and I know any second he'll be touching just the right spot.

Maybe it was only the cold, but I could feel myself starting to shake as Sheila told me she was going to find out which of the six Jesus guys had been transmitting the personal message. "I've got some money saved," she said, "I'll ride the bus. I don't know which one it is, but I'll find out. This is something I have to do."

Somehow I couldn't imagine poor Sheila alone, hanging around bus depots with transients and losers in dingy cities all across creation. I guess that's when it first came to me that we should take my car. The next thing I knew I heard myself blurt out real fast and loud—a thirteen-year-old asking for permission to date an older boy and stay out past midnight—that I'd go with her.

Sheila didn't say anything for a minute, but as she sat staring through the dirty windshield at the lights that spelled out TOPPER'S in big red neon letters, and underneath that, in smaller script, "good eats," I could see the tears again, along with the smile. Then she turned and embraced me. "I had a dream about all this," she said. "We were sitting together in the car and you said exactly those same words."

"No!"

"Yes. And then you said 'no!' just like you just did."

Since afterward, in her dream, the two of us had left the car, knelt on the blacktop of the parking lot, and prayed, we figured we ought to do that next. Though I hadn't been to church in years—not since I was a kid and we all went for Christmas—strike me dead if I'm lying, but I never felt so holy, exalted, afraid, and full of spirit as I did then, scraping my knees against the pavement with Sheila beside me mumbling prayers I'd never heard before.

About ten minutes into our session, a trucker named Bill I'd been dating pulled his rig behind my car and left it idling. "Jesus, Mary!" he called out, as he swung around the door and hopped down from the side rail, his cowboy boots thumping on the blacktop. He was holding a tire iron in his hand. As he stared at us he began to chuckle. "For a second I thought you was givin' some dude head the way you're kneeling there," he said. "What the hell are you two doing?"

"We're praying, smart-ass," I told him.

"Yeah, right," he laughed, throwing his big, woolly chin into the air. "You, praying. Now I've heard it all." Suddenly my piety turned into fury. For a second I considered grabbing the tire iron out of his hand and bringing it down hard onto his thick neck, but before even the mental picture was complete, Sheila touched my arm.

"Would you like to join us?" she asked.

"Oh no, not me, thanks," he said, taking a step back and crossing his arms over his chest. He turned to me with wide eyes. "Listen, baby, you gonna be home later?" he asked. "Maybe after I get something to eat I'll come knocking."

"Don't bother," I told him, "Sheila and I are busy."
Bill shook his head and retreated to his rig, mumbling
"I'll be damned" under his breath.

After he'd pulled away in a cloud of diesel fumes,
Sheila told me we should watch the videotape. "I sent
the television station a hundred dollars," she explained.
"I told them I needed a copy of the program fast." We
got back into the car. "The tape will be waiting for us.
I know it," Sheila said. As I put the car into gear my
cheeks were stinging, as though someone had slapped
me.

I know what that feels like, too, because my husband had done it to me once when he was drunk. We'd
been at our Friday night bowling league and he'd been
draining beers all evening. When I suggested he give
me the keys to the car, he pushed me roughly from the
driver's side door. "Just get the fuck in and shut up," he
snapped. At home he said he didn't like the way men
looked at me. "You should damn well have the decency
to wear pants when you're bowling. You reach down
for your ball and everyone gets a free goddamned
show," he said. When I told him I didn't care as long as
my audience found it interesting, the son-of-a-bitch
back-handed me hard across my face. It was the first
time in months he'd touched me. And a slap in the

chops wasn't exactly what I'd had in mind. Anyway, that did it. When Dan came home from work the next day he found his key no longer fit the lock and his clothes, balls, guns and fishing gear were piled up at the end of our driveway.

He was so pissed that he threw his stuff in the bed of his truck and burned rubber down the street. The next day, when he phoned from some bar wanting to talk, I told him I wasn't a punching bag. He asked me to think it over, but I said I already had. And except for one time a couple weeks later when the police took him off in handcuffs after he came around drunk and tried to shoot the lock off the front door of the trailer, he's left me alone ever since. I think we both knew there wasn't much between us, though neither would admit it. The truth is we'd been fussing and picking at one other for quite a while.

Our marriage was a lot like others I've seen. Dan bitched every chance he got—complained about everything from my cooking to the way I never ironed his shirts. The damned things were permanent press, for God's sake. I told him he wanted a mother, not a wife. It got uglier still on the weekends, when he'd want me to sit on some lake shore with a bunch of hopeless women and their kids while he and his sun-burned buddies raced boats and crushed beer cans against their foreheads. "How come I get the impression you don't like my friends?" he asked me once as we were driving home after a long weekend at Lake Isabella.

"Because I don't," I told him. He shot me as hateful a look as I'd ever seen. I was never good at keeping my tongue rolled, so while I was at it I told him I hated football and bowling, too. His hand squeezed the ball on the end of the stick shift between us.

"You're a selfish bitch who don't like much of nothing," he sneered. I suppose he was right: I didn't like much about my life with him.

No doubt we married too young and had too little in common for it to last. When I think back, I can't see why I did it, except that he was my first, and the sexual feeling was so strong I thought it was love—thought that it had something to do with him instead of me. We started dating in high school, and soon we were rutting in the back seat of his car every chance we got. For the first time in my life I felt really alive.

After graduation, Dan got a job pumping gas while I went two years to community college. I had a knack for it, and made good marks in just about every course I tried. I could have done anything, as my mother always said. Instead, I ended up serving slop at Toppers, a princess with a bee-hive hair-do locked in a tower of pink and orange vinyl.

Though I'd planned on transfering to a four-year school to get my degree in journalism, after Danny got himself a better job driving a truck for a beverage distribution company, he asked me to marry him. For some damned reason I ordered the cheapest thing on the menu. My parents were against the marriage, of course, which only seemed to make it more exciting for me. After all, I was tired of skinny-dipping in the back of a car. I wanted my own bed.

Even my friends tried to tell me I was making a mistake. But at that age you're more apt to listen to your heart than your head—even if it turns out later that it wasn't your heart at all you were hearing, just some dumb, scared part of yourself singing weakly in the darkness. My best friend Fanny told me straight to my face I'd be sorry. "You marry that bum and in two years he'll expect you to clap your little hands and laugh every time he farts at the dinner table."

At the time I thought she was jealous and just being cruel, but now I can see she was right. For her part, Fanny worked on her Barbie doll appearance and waited until she found an older man, a wealthy tooth doctor named Stan, who owns a string of discount dentistry clinics. Though I've always thought that Stan resembles a mole, he treats Fanny like a queen. Now she lives in a big house up on a hill, belongs to a tennis club and drives a red sports car. When she's bored she plays credit cards.

Not that I envy Fanny her life. I don't. In fact, there's nothing I'd hate worse than putting on a baby doll nightgown and crawling into bed every night with Mole Man. Rich or not, the guy gives me the creeps. And he may be good to her in some ways, but he sure as hell isn't faithful. Once, at a big New Year's Eve party at their house, Stan got sloppy and backed me into a corner while I was mixing strawberry Margaritas. Before I could stop him he was kissing me and grabbing my tits. Finally, I pushed him away. Another minute of that and I'd have kneed the bastard in the balls. After that I stopped going to him for treatment, although Fanny had arranged a special discount. I didn't want him hovering anywhere near my open mouth.

At any rate, I wish I would have heeded Fanny's warning about Dan, for soon after the wedding, I learned that college was out forever. Instead of something as abstract as a degree, Dan argued that we needed a tract house, a fiberglass boat with speed stripes, and a yard full of kids. So I got a job serving slop and we settled for a double-wide in a trailer park. Eventually, our differences made us jittery. We dropped an armful of years the way a hung-over busboy loses a stack of dishes. Though I never mentioned it, ever since the doctor told us I couldn't have a baby, I knew Dan had been fucking women he picked up in bars. Rich or poor, some things are definitely equal.

Whenever I think about my marriage, my mind flashes on the same image: I am standing next to my new husband, dressed in white lace, wearing a big smile. I'm still clutching my wedding bouquet in my hands and I am so nervous and happy at once that I have to pee. But I don't want to leave, because everyone is swarming around us, kissing me or shaking Dan's hand and slapping him on the back. I don't know why, but for some reason I look through the crowd and see a woman sitting alone on a folding chair in the garden chapel behind us. It's my mother and I see that she is crying. At the time I think it's because she is happy.

Sometimes our thoughts get tangled so that everything seems upside down. Praying with Sheila was like a slap that made me happy. I didn't make any more sense of it that night than I did of my mother's tears at my wedding.

On the way to her apartment Sheila remained silent. "Are you okay?" I finally asked.

"Oh, yes," she said, "I'm thinking about the video tape." Sure enough, when we arrived we found a package on the doorstep. Sheila's hand shook as she fumbled in her purse for her key. Inside, I poured us tumblers of whiskey and sat down on the couch as Sheila kicked off her shoes and loaded the cassette. I was still shivering and the whiskey felt fine going down.

I could hardly sit still as we watched that show and I finished my drink before Sheila had even touched hers. On the one hand it was pretty much what you'd expect—a bunch of whackos claiming to be God or God's messengers entertaining the bored insomniacs in TV-land. That part was okay. But Sheila's reaction got to me. The smile. The tears. The labored breathing and eyes rolling back in the head. The stream of babble. And finally, the shaky arms reaching out toward the television, palms up.

I stood up and embraced her as tight as a straight-jacket. Her hard sobbing told me she was choking or having a seizure. I shook her, tipped her head, held her whiskey to her lips, poured some, and forced her to swallow. "Jesus Christ, Sheila!" I screamed, "stop it!" Finally, I slapped her. I didn't know what else to do. She was making me hysterical.

As Sheila collapsed against me, I heard a voice cut the stillness. The television behind me seemed to be radiating a hot aura of electricity, a pulse that filled the room. Soft and insistent, the voice pressed in from all sides: "The ultimate gift is sacrifice." I turned just as the screen flashed to a commercial for disposable diapers. My heart pounded as I watched two toddlers racing across a kitchen floor on their hands and knees, their white-diapered behinds bobbing furiously as their stubby legs pumped. I gasped as a hand touched my shoulder.

Sheila smiled at me. "I'm certain now," she said, her voice low and steady. I saw myself reflected in her eyes. Gently she squeezed then patted my shoulder, her hand fluttering towards me. "We'll leave tomorrow." I nodded, grabbed my purse and walked out the door.

Driving home I wondered what I'd got myself into. Sure, I'd trashed my life, but was that any reason to run away? It was as if I'd volunteered to work the graveyard shift just because I'd scalded a customer during the day. Yet I felt strangely elated. "What the hell," I said out loud. "What have I got to lose?"

I tilted my head back and set my chin as though my profile were being photographed. I unrolled the window so that my hair would blow wild around my face. I held that pose and imagined a man's voice crooning: "Serenity. The scent of an angel."

The next day I woke early and, instead of sitting on the porch drinking coffee in the morning sunlight, I cleaned my kitchen, emptied the refrigerator and put two loads of laundry into the coin-operated machine before most people had even left for work. Later I went to the bank and tried to close my savings account, but the teller whined about checks that hadn't cleared.

"Just figure it out," I told her. "I want as much of my money as you'll give me." When the manager stood in back of the teller and asked if there was a problem, I raised my voice. "I just want the money that's in my account," I repeated. They both looked at me like I was pointing a gun at them.

Next I took my car to a tire shop, where I bought a new set of radials and had them fix the brakes. On my way home, at the manager's office, I paid three months rent on my trailer park space. Then I phoned to suspend the utilities and phone service, and asked the post office to hold my mail. Finally, I called Rick, the day manager at the restaurant, and told him I wouldn't be coming back to work.

The line was silent as he waited for me to say more. But I had nothing to add. "First Sheila, now you. Is this some kind of joke?" he finally asked.

"It's no joke," I said, smiling at the anxiety I detected in his voice. It pleased me to make him squirm. After all, Rick was a deep-dish asshole, the kind of jerk who thought he was superior to the waitresses. He did whatever he could to make our lives miserable, including stealing tips from us, which created resentment and hostility. Most of us called him "P-Rick" behind his back.

"You two are really leaving me in the lurch, you know," he complained. "What am I going to do at crunch time tonight with only three waitresses?"

"That's your problem," I said. "Just make sure you mail me my check."

"Bitch," I heard him mutter as I hung up.

Finally, I began to pack. I threw an old ice chest and sleeping bag in the car, along with my suitcase, some camping equipment and a big box of odds and ends. When I'd finished loading, I called Sheila. A recorded message informed me that the number had been disconnected.

When I got to her apartment, I found the door wide open. Sheila was standing in the middle of an empty space, a suitcase at her feet, her large purse flung back over her shoulder, a set of keys in her hand. She told me the Goodwill truck had hauled all her things away. "You mean you gave them everything?" I asked.

"I won't be needing much anymore," she said.

After setting the keys on the kitchen counter, Sheila picked up her suitcase and walked outside and down the stairs without looking back. I followed her to the parking lot. As she neared my car, Sheila dropped her bag on the pavement and rummaged in her purse. "Oh, yes," she said, "I want you to hold onto this for us." She pressed a huge wad of rolled-up bills into my hand. "Put it someplace safe," she said.

I considered dropping the money down the front of my dress so that the bills would nestle in my cleavage. I'd done that before with tips, but only to make the truckers laugh. Instead, the money still in my fist, I unlocked the car and pushed the driver's seat forward, my eyes focused on the ornament in the rear window— a fuzzy brown dog that sat on its haunches, ready to bounce its head with motion sickness.

Years earlier I'd bought what used to be called an economy car—which at the time meant Japanese— from a guy who babbled on about what a great deal I was getting. "Low miles," he kept repeating, "hate to let it go so cheap." It turned out he was selling it because it reminded him of his mother, who he'd buried two weeks prior. It had been the old lady's car and he'd left the dog in it. Somehow I didn't have the heart to get rid of it either. After a while I came to like it, and whenever

I walked to the car after work, it always made me smile.

As I scrambled into the cramped back seat I remembered how once when Fanny's twins were riding in the back seat they pulled the dog's head off its body. As the head rolled onto the floor, Fanny reached to slap each kid in turn. "I'm so sorry, hon," she told me, "these brats break everything." But when we got to the mall I rescued the head and simply popped it back in place.

Kneeling on the sun-warmed vinyl of the rear seat, I grabbed the dog by the ears and gently jerked the head loose. Then I set the cash next to me on the seat. The stack of large bills curled at each end: Jacksons, Jeffersons, Grants. For a moment I just stared at it. I'd never seen so much money in one place before. I was so busy flipping through the stack that I nearly hit my head on the ceiling when Sheila tapped on the window and pressed her round face against the glass. She smiled down over me as I rolled the bills into a tight cylinder and dropped them into the neck hole of the dog. Then I popped the head back on and pushed it once with my finger to set it bouncing. Outside, Sheila clapped her hands and giggled like a child.

Once we'd put Sheila's suitcase in the trunk, we got into the car and drove south. As usual, a thick broth of fog and haze hung over the valley, obscuring visibility. We laughed together nervously at the odd signs along the road that led out of town. "This is a sad place," I said, as we passed a junkyard for tractors and other farm equipment, "and I've spent my whole life here." Sheila cocked her head slightly. I could tell what she was thinking: There are no sad places, only sad people. I loved her for not saying it.

As we drove, Sheila explained how she'd pestered people at the television station all week until, finally, an associate producer told her how to locate the guests on the program. According to the producer, privacy wasn't an issue, as they'd each signed a clearance allowing the station to give out information in care of their various ministries.

"I called John Peter Paul Lord's agent in Los Angeles," she told me. "He said the band is playing every night for the next two weeks at a nightclub in Hollywood. When I mentioned seeing the show on television, he was very helpful. He invited us to attend a performance. 'JPP is going to love this,' he told me."

"You mean we're starting with the rock and roll guy?" I said, slapping my hand against my forehead. On television it had seemed obvious that his gospel, which he'd called "post-punk apocalyptic" was nothing more than publicity for his band.

"It's important for us to begin with him," Sheila explained. "He's returning to England as soon as the band is done playing in Hollywood. They may not be back for years." I wanted to say something snide, but my throat suddenly felt thick and closed, so I simply nodded. Sheila stared out the window and sighed.

By the time we got to Los Angeles it was late afternoon, hot, and so smoggy we could barely see the mountains in the brown distance. As we drew closer to the center of the city, traffic clotted. All around us people sat in their cars, listening to radios. We jerked along for over an hour, following the big green signs to North Hollywood, where we found a motel with a swimming pool.

That night we slept with the cooler blowing. At about two in the morning, over the noise of the fan we heard loud voices arguing, then, a few minutes later, gun shots in the parking lot. Police cars pulled up with sirens blaring. Red lights flashed through our curtains. Outside, people stood around talking to the cops. Tens minutes later the parking lot was again deserted. Then, an hour later, the whole thing started up again.

In the morning I looked into the bathroom mirror and saw that my eyes looked red and puffy. "We better see if we can find that club and try to meet Lord tonight," I told Sheila.

It turned out we weren't even in Hollywood, which was someplace "over the hill," as the guy at the gas station put it. "You'll know you're there because you can see the sign, those big letters up along the ridge." So we checked out of the motel and headed for Sunset Boulevard. Eventually we stumbled upon the Axe and Rose, where a voice muffled by the closed door informed us that the club wasn't open. We'd have to come back in the evening and pay a cover charge.

"Can't we buy our tickets now?" Sheila asked, cupping her hand and yelling into the black void of the door. "We don't want to miss the show."

The voice laughed. "Just get here some time between nine and ten and you'll get in. Once you've paid, you can get your hand stamped so you can leave and come back later when things pick up. That's what most people do."

After we'd checked into a motel on Sunset, a few miles from the club, we ate lunch in a coffee shop that served the worst decaff I'd ever tasted. I wanted the waitress to brew a fresh pot, but instead Sheila told the girl everything was fine. Though I made a big show of pouring two packets of artificial sweetener into the cup, stirring it with my spoon, sipping once then pushing the cup and saucer to the center of the table,

Sheila didn't seem to notice. When we left, she laid down a huge tip. "Such a poor soul," Sheila explained, waving to the waitress as we pushed through the door and stepped back into the blast-furnace heat.

When we returned to our room, I asked Sheila what she planned to wear to the club. She showed me a white dress that looked like something an eastern European bride might don for a country wedding. I begged her to go shopping with me. "We're going to need to look attractive," I told her, but she shook her head and said she'd rather take a nap. Before I left, she handed me two hundred dollar bills from her wallet. "We've got plenty more in the dog," she insisted when I tried to refuse the money.

I had wanted to go to Beverly Hills, and even mapped out my route in advance. Nevertheless, lost amid the sprawl of the city, I ended up in Westwood, an area crowded with shops, restaurants and movie theaters, near the university. After driving around for half an hour, I finally gave up on the idea of finding a parking space on the street and paid to enter a lot. I put the ticket in my purse and took off walking.

In front of a book shop a mime was imitating passersby. Farther down the street I entered a boutique specializing in accessories: matching purses and shoes, scarf, hat and glove sets, colorful glass beads and handsome costume jewelry. I tried on a black silk hat adorned with a pheasant feather and a lace veil that hung over the eyes, and winked at myself in the mirror. But when I checked the price tag I quickly returned it to its foam head and left the store. Finally I located a department store.

On the second floor I found a section where the colors and fabrics whistled at me from the racks. I gathered up an armful of clothes that knew how to flirt and whisper about close fits and took them with me into the dressing room. After trying on half a dozen outfits, I bought a red sleeveless silk blouse, a black leather skirt, and fishnet pantyhose. At a shoe store down the street I picked out a pair of red pumps. I had wanted to get my hair and make-up done, too, but the money was gone and I didn't feel right about robbing the dog for more. Instead, I stopped in a bakery for a chocolate eclair.

By the time I got back to the motel it was already getting late. Sheila and I took turns in the bathroom, then dressed for the evening. When she was finished, Sheila sat on the edge of the bed and watched me try to fix my hair. I finally piled it loosely on my head. Then I began my make-up. Reflected in the mirror I could see her watching. I painted my lower lip, then pressed my lips together, kissing. "You want to borrow some lipstick?" Sheila shook her head and smiled.

At eight-thirty we arrived at the Axe and Rose. The other people in line were young, mostly in their late teens and early twenties, and a few of them looked at us strangely. Sheila was wearing her white dress with a powder blue shawl and a pair of red shoes with bows and sparkles like Dorothy's in *The Wizard of Oz*. One girl in line, wearing a black skirt, ripped tights and a lacy black bra with no blouse, glared at us. She had a shaved head, black eye make-up, tattooed arms and chest and chains hanging from her pierced ears and nose. The way she rocked from side to side and waved her hands made her seem drunk or insane. When she was sure we'd noticed her, she threw back her head and laughed, as she stroked her enormous breasts, squeezing them together and cupping them in her hands. I noticed Sheila's lips moving slightly, though I couldn't make out what she was saying to herself.

After we paid the cover charge, a bouncer in a tight t-shirt with huge arms grunted and stamped our hands. He didn't bother to check our i.d. Inside, the sound was deafening, though the band had not yet taken the stage. I thought I might have to leave before the show even started. Flashing colored lights blinked on and off, the air smelled of stale beer and smoke, and everywhere I looked kids in ripped jeans bumped into each other, yelling. Sheila was motionless, as if paralyzed. Putting my hand against her back, I guided her to an empty table near the back wall. A waitress with dark circles under her eyes took our order. Fifteen minutes later she brought a bottle of beer for me and a dirty glass of soda for Sheila.

A long time passed before the band came out and began setting up. They wore tight black leather pants and had longer hair than most of the girls in the audience. When the guitar player struck a loud chord the house lights dimmed. A man in a purple velvet tuxedo walked on stage and grabbed a microphone. "Welcome ladies and gentlemen to the Axe and Rose," he announced, "Tonight I have the special pleasure of introducing you to the apoc-rock sound of one of the most divine bands in this or any other world. Direct from London, I give you Lorrrrd Allll-mighty."

Instantly the band started making a terrible racket and people screamed as a spotlight revealed a skinny young man in a white robe who was crawling across the stage with a wooden crucifix on his back. On his head he wore a crown of barbed wire and his black hair and beard were matted with thick paste, his robe stained dark with what appeared to be blood. He moved along the stage on his knees, then stood up and tossed the cross to the floor, where it made a terrific crash.

Standing at the edge of the raised platform, arms outstretched, he worked the crowd. Suddenly he reached for the microphone and began wailing.

> *From on all high now hear what I say:*
> *Get on your knees baby, time to pray,*
> *If it's good I might reward your bad behavior,*
> *'cause I'm your Lord and I'm your savior.*

I looked at Sheila and saw that she had closed her eyes and was pressing the tips of her fingers against her temples. I touched her hand and asked if she wanted to leave. Before she could answer, a jet of cigarette smoke blew into our faces. "Hey, babe, you wanna dance?" I looked up. The girl from the line outside, the one with the shaved head, was leaning over the table.

"Look, we're busy right now," I started, but she cut me off.

"Who the fuck's talking to you, hag?" she snorted. "Don't think I give a shit about your little lover's spat, 'cause I don't. I'm just asking hot-cheeks here if she wants to get on the floor with me. How about it?" She took another puff on her cigarette and blew a ring of smoke through her brittle laughter.

I grabbed the beer bottle in front of me by the neck and started to pull back from the table, but Sheila stopped me with a touch on the shoulder. "Thank you very much for asking," Sheila said softly, "but I'd rather just listen to the music for now."

"I'd rather just listen to the music," the girl whined, imitating Sheila's voice through her nose. She tossed the burning cigarette onto our table and pinched her nipples through her bra with both hands. "You know, you're one butt-ugly dyke," she said to Sheila. "And you got a lot of nerve coming in here like somebody's fairy-fucking godmother." Then she leaned over the table, pulled her bra cup down and slapped Sheila across the cheek with her big dangling breast. "Adios, bitch," she called back over her shoulder as she walked away.

I had to go to the bathroom, but I was afraid to leave Sheila alone, afraid, too, at what I might find there, so I crossed my legs and sat very still as John Peter Paul Lord screamed into the second set. *So much pain and so much sorrow, Let's live tonight like there's no tomorrow.* I took a ball-point pen from my purse and wrote "Can we leave now?" on my napkin and pushed it across to Sheila. She motioned for my pen and I handed it to her. "I need to talk to him," she wrote.

The last hour before closing a number of men asked me to dance, but I turned them all down. I was still crossing my legs to hold off the flood. Then three young guys in jeans and flannel shirts invited themselves to our table and sat down. "What's your name?" one screamed into my ear.

"Petra," I yelled back, "I'm an exchange student." A round of fresh drinks appeared at the table, then another. At one point I thought I overheard Sheila talking about carpentry. Her companions nodded gravely. Meanwhile, I laughed, smiled and flirted just enough to stay busy. Finally the management announced last call and the band played its final number. The lights came on. People hooted and pressed toward the exit. I ran to the rest room.

When I got back, the guys were still buzzing around Sheila, looking strangely determined, as if they understood how pathetic the situation was but couldn't, despite that realization, resist going on. After we'd declined their offer of drinks at their place or coffee somewhere out, Sheila and I headed for the door leading back stage. No one stopped us, so we stood for a moment at the entrance to the backstage lounge. The band members were talking to a few admirers in a room whose only furnishings were an old couch and a mirror over a long counter. Amplifiers, speakers and other electrical equipment were piled in every corner.

Finally Sheila pushed through and entered the

room, heading for the lead singer, who was talking to a man dressed in a baggy pin-striped suit and a girl in a polka-dot mini dress with a matching bow on her head. I followed slowly, my hand touching the wall, as if I were walking among the ruined props and half-painted backdrops of a theatrical nightmare.

I watched as Sheila broke into the conversation. John Peter Paul laughed out loud, his head tilting. "Ketchup," he said, still laughing. The others also laughed. A moment later Lord offered Sheila a drink from a bottle of Jack Daniels. She waved her hand in front of her. Then the man in the suit shook hands with the singer and the girl bent forward to peck his cheek. "Who's that you've got with you, luv?" Lord asked Sheila, motioning to me as the other two waved good-bye on their way to the door.

"That's my friend, Mary," Sheila said, grabbing my hand and pulling me closer.

"Another Mary, then, is it?"

"That's right." I looked at him and smiled. "Quite a show."

He laughed. "We've toned it down for the States," he said. "I was just telling the other Mary how we did a whole crucifixion number live one time in Birmingham. Hired footballers and dressed 'em up as Roman soldiers. One actually bloody nailed me to the cross with ten penny spikes. There's no fakin' *that* I'll tell you. Of course I'd had x-rays taken beforehand and marked the right spots. Still hurt like hell. That's how I got the stigmata."

"Stigmata?"

He held up his hands. "Yeah, the bleedin' wounds in me hands and feet. Band used to be called Stigmata, but then we figured a change of name would take us deeper into the J.C. thing." I looked around. Somehow Sheila had slipped away. I couldn't see her anywhere.

"Originally, we called the band Wolfpack. Tried to work up a whole U-boat motif. You know, submarines and such rot." He took a pull from the bottle, then offered it to me. "We wanted an easy association with the underground. Well, underwater, anyway. I used to wear a bleedin' navy turtleneck and commander's hat I bought at a replica shop in London—military gear. Had a periscope we'd hang from the ceiling and a real klaxon sound off the command to dive. Good effect, that one. And our drummer had freighter silhouettes tattooed all over his chest. Used to come on stage without a shirt till he got himself pneumonia playing a drafty club. No choice but to let Roger go after that. Damn shame, too. Pathetic, really. Near the end, the poor bloke could hardly hold onto the sticks." I looked over his shoulder, still searching for Sheila.

"You know, you're a lovely little ducky," Lord said, touching my hair. When I didn't shy away, he slipped his arm around my waist and pulled me close. With his free hand he tipped the bottle. As he drank I stepped back so that I was facing him again.

"This new bit has worked out much better, all right," he said, wiping his mouth on his sleeve. "It's a damned sight closer to the myth, I suppose. The source of original sin. If rock 'n roll's a holy terror, better to find the pulse of hysteria, ecstasy, tribal rhythm. That's what it's all about, now, isn't it, luv?"

"If you say so." I tried to look pleasant. He smiled back, showing a row of stained teeth.

"Say, I've a video of that Birmingham show at the hotel. It's a bit of all right if you don't mind me saying so."

"I've got to find my friend," I told him.

He winked. "Right. I'll wait here for you then, luv."

When I returned to the main room, I saw that the club was empty except for some workers who were sweeping the floors and stacking the chairs on top of the tables. Back in the lounge I told John Peter Paul she'd disappeared.

"I wouldn't worry about that one," he said, "she's

probably gone home is all. She told me the show gave her a head spin."

"But she doesn't have the keys to the car," I said.

"She'll get on all right."

The next thing I knew I was in a rented limo, on my way to John Peter Paul Lord's hotel room, where I passed the night in sin with the rock and roll Messiah. And for all his concert-time posturing and screeching, I found him to be gentle, considerate, civilized and funny. He could even carry a tune, which he did when he sang a lullaby before I left the next morning. When he wasn't playing Jesus, JPP had a tremendous sense of humor. And to be honest, he wasn't half bad in the sack either, though he didn't make me see God there any more than he did on stage.

We never got around to watching the videotape. Instead, he dropped the Cockney and told me about his childhood among the privileged merchant class in England—his given name was Jonathan Peter Pinch-cock. He told me he'd once been a student of Political Science and Social Philosophy who had wanted to help change the lives of those who worked in the grim, out-moded factories his family had controlled for genera-tions.

"It's ghastly how those people exist, really," he said. "As a child I was kept from all that. We lived on an estate, you see, with proper servants. I remember the first time I ever saw them—the faceless masses, I mean. Still a bit of a tike, I was riding in my father's car. For some reason the nanny was bringing me downtown to the old man's office. I'm not sure why. Anyway, it was a rainy winter day and I'd cut a bit of a fuss about not wanting to wrap up in my slicker—I was apt to throw terrific fits as a child—which had caused us to be late. By the time she'd got me properly dressed and into the car, the nanny was in a panic, for it simply wouldn't do to keep my father waiting. So all along the way, she kept pleading with the driver to gas it. With the roads wet there was nothing much he could do. Finally he told her he'd worked up a short cut. The problem was, it took us right through the blight—those sections of the city I'd never seen, including a rough spot where the workers lived. I remember pressing my face against the window of the car and staring out at sodden chaps in filthy rags with stooped backs and faces like creased newsprint, ratty old tenements, gloomy streets laid out one miserable corner after another. Later, when I told my pop what I'd seen, he laughed. 'That's poor folks, is all, Johnny,' he said, 'it's nothing to be scared of.'

"Anyway, they've nothing much to live for, these people, aside from the pub. And the younger ones know they won't have even the life their parents have.

For them there's not a scrap of hope."

"So you decided to offer them old-fashioned salvation?" I said.

"Not exactly. It was more like one day I realized I was on the road to becoming just another bloody absurd professor pleading for some kind of bleeding-heart social reform—the kind of tweedy bugger who'd never missed tea in his life. I got to the point where I didn't fancy myself that kind of chap, that's all. So I got out. Simple as that. Left school and went into the streets without a plan in my head."

"And then?"

"Well, it took some time. At that point I had no idea what I was about. For a while I drifted without much direction at all. Worked a piece here and there, mostly rough trades, and spent my time drinking and throwing darts. I didn't want anyone to guess my background, so I mostly kept my mouth shut and my stomach full of bitters. At the time I was living in the lowest kind of flat. I'd taken up with a gal I'd met in a pub, and what little money I had we gave for drugs. It was damned pathetic, I'm sure, though still a sight better, I thought, than what I'd been doing before.

"Not long after, I heard about something riotous happening in the clubs, so I thought 'why not?' And from the first night I knew the punkers were onto something. There was all this anger, see, so thick you could feel it pressing down like fog on the streets. The desperation was real and the punks found a way to meet it. Of course they had no focus and no solutions—it was all bloody nihilism and anarchy—but the energy, the acknowledgment, was there all the same.

"About that time I met up with Jimmy—you saw him tonight. He's our lead guitarist and the real creative force behind our band. Though the two of us work together on the theatrical elements, it's Jimmy who writes the music and most of the lyrics. He's a bleedin' genius, that one. Learned to play the piano at the age of four and the violin the year after. Went into the conservatory at fifteen. But like me, in the end he couldn't crack it. Got a gorgeous voice, too, a trained tenor. And here's the funny part. We first met in a pub, of course. I was so blasted I could hardly balance on the stool. Next thing I know this bloke who looks like he's just plugged into a socket pops onto the chair beside me and after a while we start talking. He tells me his name's Jimmy and he's putting together a band but lacks a singer. After another pint he asks how I'd like to have a go at it. I told him right off I don't know the first thing about music, that I'm not even the type to belt out in the shower. 'You ought to be perfect, then, mate,' he says.

"Sure enough, all he really wanted was someone to scream about on stage, since he couldn't do it himself. You see, all that classical training had ruined his voice for screaming and for him ugly sounds didn't come easy. But he was right enough about me. As soon as I got over being self-conscious, I was good enough for it. Of course, being a pair of bleedin' intellectual drop-outs, we couldn't keep from refining the whole concept. That's how we went from Wolfpack to Lord Almighty. And Jimmy's been giving me voice lessons on the side."

About that time I began to realize that John might talk all night, in which case I wouldn't get any sleep. So as he paused for breath, I rested my head against his shoulder. A minute later we were kissing, and an hour after that John was snoring beside me in bed. But despite the good time I'd had with him, I couldn't sleep; as I lay there I kept wondering about Sheila. I hoped she hadn't got herself into trouble.

The next morning, as I rode the taxi back to pick up my car, I felt like the worst kind of tramp. Here it was only a couple of days after I'd set off with my friend on a spiritual quest and already I had ditched her to sleep with the first Jesus we'd come to. Worse, I'd let her walk miles along Sunset Boulevard in Hollywood, alone after midnight in her white dress and red sparkle shoes. It was a low thing to have done. I only hoped Sheila would be waiting for me in the motel room when I got there. Maybe she'd slap my face and send me back to Bakersfield. That's what I would have done. But I knew she'd never do anything like that, and somehow my knowing it increased my guilt.

I decided to stop at a donut shop before going back to the motel. Showing up with a pink box of buttermilk bars, raised glazed, and jelly-filled, along with two large cups of steaming coffee, would help absolve my sins. I certainly wasn't counting on being harassed by the police, though that's what happened. I had just got out of my car and started toward the donut stand when an officer in a black and white cruiser waved me over. Maybe I did look strange for early Sunday morning, but for all they knew I could have been on my way to church. In fact, that's exactly what I told them. "Some women like to dress up for God," I said.

His partner, a tall blond guy wearing dark sunglasses, got out of the car. I watched as he fingered his nightstick. "As long as you aren't planning to turn tricks during mass, we won't have any problem with it," he told me. Both of them snorted. Then the one in the cruiser asked for my identification. "Is that your car, Ma'am?" the tall one added, pointing. When I nodded, he asked for the registration. I swear they just wanted me to walk across the parking lot so they could see me shake it. So I did it for them, clicking my heels, wiggling my ass, and bouncing my tits all the way. Before they let me go, they suggested I might head back to Bakersfield as soon as my vacation was over. "I'll be leaving early," I told them. "The people here aren't real friendly." They followed me for a mile or so down Sunset Boulevard.

Over the past few hours I'd acted like a tramp and been mistaken for a whore. Suddenly I found myself back at the motel full of guilt, but without the coffee and donuts. All I could think of was grabbing Sheila and begging for forgiveness. I saw myself falling to my knees, crying. I was glad to be wearing sunglasses.

Since I'd left the key to the room with Sheila, I knocked on the door and stood outside, waiting for her to open. I was ready to knock a second time when I heard the dead bolt turn and the door cracked open the width of the safety chain. A narrow slit of strange face stared out. "I must have the wrong room," I mumbled.

"Come in," the face said. I heard the chain slide along the metal track, then the door opened wide. "Mary's taking a shower." My eyes moved from the shaved head to the black lace bra and the tattoos. It was the abusive girl from the club. "Remember me?" she said, extending her hand, "I'm Chiquita." Cautiously I took her hand in mine as I stepped into the room.

"I'm. . . I'm Mary," I said. She squeezed my hand hard and pumped rigorously.

"I know. We've been expecting you." I looked around and saw that there were two other teenage girls sitting on the bed watching cartoons on television. One was a tiny Vietnamese, the other a pale girl of no more than fourteen, with blotchy skin and thin blond hair. They smiled at me shyly.

"Hello," I said.

"These are my friends Nan and Sid." Chiquita motioned toward them with her chin. "We all came here together."

"Yeah," said Nan, the Asian girl, "Mary said it's okay for us if we stay." She smiled again. Just then Sheila entered the room, dressed in a pink slip, her hair wrapped in a motel towel.

"Your friend's crazy," Chiquita said, pointing. "Look at her." Sheila stood with her back to the dressing mirror and her hands on her hips. She started to laugh but, seeing my face, stopped and crossed her arms.

"These girls had to have somewhere to stay," she explained. "They've run away from home. They were hungry and needed a shower and a place to sleep."

For a minute everyone was silent. On television the

coyote slammed into a sheer cliff then disappeared in a puff of smoke in the canyon below. My eyes went from Sheila to the three girls, then back to Sheila. "Look, how did this . . . I mean, I'm confused," I said.

Chiquita cleared her throat, then struck a match which she touched to the cigarette dangling from her mouth. "We were working Sunset, waiting for johns, when we saw the Good Witch of the West here walking along in her white dress with that blue thing over her head. It was too fucking weird," she said, exhaling a plume of gray smoke. "I wanted to rip that little purse right out of her hand, push her arm up behind her back and maybe hurt her bad, but she walked right up to us and started talking. 'It's a such a nice night,' she said, 'but I didn't have dinner so I'm going to get a snack. Would you girls like to go across the street with me for a donut?' A fucking donut! Can you believe it?"

"We all went with her," said Nan, showing crooked teeth through her smile.

"They were very hungry," Sheila added. "Nan told me she hadn't eaten in two days. So, after the donuts, I took them to the nice coffee shop where you and I had lunch and I bought them each a hamburger."

"And then you came here?" I asked, digging through my suitcase for clean clothes.

"Yes, I invited them to share the room. The four of

us had a wonderful time."

"You did?"

"Yes. We talked about all kinds of things."

"Right," I said, pushing past Chiquita toward the bathroom. "Listen, Sheila, all this is a bit much for me to digest right now. I'm exhausted. So if you'll excuse me, I'm going to take a shower. Then I think we'd better get our stuff packed and check out of here."

"Yes," Sheila nodded, "I already told the girls we're leaving today for Arizona. Chiquita asked if she could come with us." I stopped suddenly and spun around.

"Come with us?"

"I've got my own money, if that's what you're thinking," Chiquita spat back at me. She grabbed a fake rabbit-fur jacket off the arm chair and waved it around in the air as if to prove she owned more than black underwear. "Mary already said it's okay." She glared at me from across the room. "Beep-beep," came a sound from the television. One of the other girls giggled nervously.

"I'll think about it," I said. Then I stepped into the bathroom, shut the door and clicked the lock behind me. Alone in the shower, I closed my eyes and stood perfectly still as the warm water washed over my head and cascaded down my back. I felt so worn out and alone that I let myself go for a good long cry.

When I finally stepped out of the bathroom, the drapes were open and the room was filled with sunlight. The key to the room and my purse were posed on top of the television. Apparently, Sheila had already carried the rest of our belongings to the car. I dug my dark sunglasses out of my purse and put them on. Then I wrapped my dirty underwear along with the blouse I'd worn the night before inside the skirt, rolled it all into a ball and tucked it under my arm.

Outside, I saw Sheila and Chiquita leaning against the car's hood as they waited for me to drop the key off at the motel office. Nan and Sid had disappeared. Eyes hidden behind the dark glasses, I walked quickly from the office to the car. My hands shook as I opened the door and slid behind the wheel. "Let's go," I said.

Sheila opened the passenger-side door and bent the seat forward while Chiquita scrambled into the back. I started the engine and pretended to concentrate on finding an acceptable radio station, settling finally on country-western music, which I suspected Chiquita would hate. Though I half expected her to complain about it, she sat quietly in the back. As I accelerated up the freeway on-ramp, I sneaked a look at her in the rearview mirror and found her humming along contentedly to herself. No one spoke until we were safely out of Los Angeles, heading up the Cajon

Pass on our way to Barstow.

By then we'd lost the last strong signal my car radio would pick up and, tired of wrestling with the static, I shut off the receiver. Suddenly Chiquita leaned forward, her hands gripping the back of my headrest, and blurted out, "So how was your date with the Almighty Lord?" For a second I ignored the question. Then, instead of answering, I turned to Sheila and said, "Look, about last night…"

"It's okay," she said. "I knew right away that he wasn't the one. But maybe for you he was." I didn't understand what she was getting at, but I nodded my head anyway, thankful that she didn't hold it against me.

"So the son of God was just another son-of-a-bitch, huh?" Chiquita whined again from the back seat. Easing off on the gas pedal slightly, I turned my head part way around and snapped at her.

"For your information, Chinchilla, or whatever your name is, Jesus Christ is not some character in a comic book." I could feel my face turning red.

"Hey, no offense intended," Chiquita said, laughing at my anger. Then, to Sheila, she added: "Maybe it's true love?"

When we got to Barstow the early afternoon sun was beating on the stretched hide of the desert. I pulled the car into a discount service station and shut off the engine. A man in a John Deere cap hobbled out of the office, looked at us, and spat on the ground. Suddenly I realized I only had a couple of dollars and some change in left in my purse. "Have you got any money on you?" I asked Sheila.

"Let me look," she said, digging through her purse. "No, I spent most of what I had last night. Those girls were pretty hungry. I guess we'll have to get some out of the dog." My heart sank. Was Sheila really dumb enough to show Chiquita the money? I watched in the mirror as Chiquita followed every word. Her face looked puzzled. Then Sheila turned around and asked her to open up the dog and get out two twenties for pocket money and one more for gas. "The head pulls right off," she said. My stomach knotted. I wanted to scream.

"So that's where you keep your cash?" Chiquita said, reaching behind her and popping the head off the fuzzy body. "What a wicked hiding place." She peeled the bills off the roll and handed them forward. "Hold on," she said, "I'm going to put my money in there, too." She seemed giddy. I watched in the rear view mirror as she pulled a couple of wrinkled twenties from the lining of the Rabbit-fur jacket and pretended to stuff them into the dog. "What's mine is yours," she said, popping the head back on again. Who did she think she was fooling? Though her back was turned, I could tell she was fumbling the money back into her bra.

I got out and unscrewed the cap to the gas tank. Outside it was as dry and hot as an open oven. My back was wet from sweating into the vinyl seat and my panties stuck to my ass. The station attendant stood off to the side and didn't offer to help pump. Instead, he leaned against the awning support pole with his arms crossed as he watched me struggle with the awkward rubber hose, which writhed in my hands like a python. Sheila got out of the car, bent over and touched her toes, then washed the windshield with a squeegee soaked in dirty water.

Then the three of us took turns using the filthy restroom. Finally, the attendant took the bill I gave him and limped to the cash box. When he handed me the change he mumbled something under his breath and spat on the ground again, this time only a few inches from my feet. He chuckled at my disgust. I hurried back to the car and started the engine. When I looked over my shoulder he was still leering. I blew him a kiss and gave him the finger. Behind me Chiquita squealed with laughter. "I love it," she said. While I waited for traffic to clear, she slipped her jeans to her knees, scrambled up the seat and pressed her naked buttocks against the rear window.

"Oh, for Christ's sake, sit down," I told her.

We pushed on to Kingman, stopping in Needles to buy sandwiches, and then along the side of the road to switch drivers. At that point Sheila took the wheel, while Chiquita moved up front and I crawled into the back, hoping I might sleep. But Sheila was uncertain behind the wheel, barely holding the car at the speed limit. Even on uphill grades the big semis kept passing us. I could feel the car shudder each time one blew by. Finally, exhausted, I closed my eyes. As I drifted into sleep I could hear Sheila talking to Chiquita. I couldn't imagine what she might be saying.

When I woke we were rolling along the main drag of a brightly-lit little city. Passing the more expensive lodgings, we drove toward the outskirts of town, where we found a run-down, L-shaped motel called "The Good Knight Inn." I made Sheila stay in the car with Chiquita while I went to register. Inside the office there was a fake suit of armor in the corner. A pair of crossed swords and a shield hung on the wall behind the desk. I filled out the paperwork and paid cash for one night. The young clerk stared at me as though he'd never seen a woman before.

Despite the name, the only medieval decoration in

our room was a framed reproduction of a painting. In the foreground of the picture several knights in full armor sat on horses as an army passed by them on the road below. One of the mounted figures—the only one without a helmet—was set off slightly from the others. This knight, who had long hair and a smooth, delicate face, held aloft a crucifix, a gesture which inspired the men marching by, some of whom were waving their weapons or had raised their hats and helmets in response. Chiquita noticed me staring at the painting.

"It's Joan," she said. When I turned to look at her she smiled. "Of Arc," she continued, "Joan of fucking Arc. They burned her alive."

While Sheila and Chiquita settled into the room, I went out to the car to retrieve the maps. While I was there, I took the money out of the dog and stuffed it inside my purse, which I set carefully on the night stand next to the bed. Since there were two double beds in the room, Sheila and I decided to bunk together, leaving the second bed for Chiquita, who admitted to snoring and thrashing around in her sleep. "I'm full of bad dreams," she explained, lighting a cigarette.

Before we turned in for the night, we looked over the maps, trying to determine exactly where we'd be going the next day. Based on the information Sheila had received from the television station, we were headed for Noxema, a town near the Painted Desert. She'd been given an address there—a place to send requests for more information. It was the only lead we had, for the man we were seeking ran an isolated commune in the desert.

"Maybe we should try to find a phone number," I suggested.

"I already checked," Sheila said. "There isn't any."

"I like communes," offered Chiquita. "I lived in one in Malibu. A place in the hills run by bikers. You could see the sun set over the ocean. They kicked me out, though, when they found out I was underage. Can't say I blame them."

"When we get to Noxema we'll ask," Sheila said. "Someone will know where he is." As Sheila talked, Chiquita, who was sitting at the little table by the window, brought a deck of cards from her purse and began cutting and shuffling.

"Up for a game?" she asked.

"No."

"Mary's tired from driving," Sheila said. "Maybe we should go to bed now."

Chiquita jumped up, threw the cards onto the floor, and launched herself into the air, landing on her back in the center of the bed, arms stretched out on either side of her. "Good idea," she said.

Despite my exhaustion, I slept poorly, flopping from stomach to back and rolling from side to side. Asleep beside me, Sheila never moved, barely seemed at times to be breathing, while in the other bed Chiquita thrashed and jumped, gnashed her teeth, snored and cursed aloud as she wandered through the maze of her psyche. Only after hours of fitful restlessness did I sleep.

The next morning Sheila and I awoke to find Chiquita gone and my purse lying open on the carpet by the door. The money was missing. Fortunately, she hadn't taken the car. I screamed at Sheila: "Goddamn it, I knew we shouldn't have let her come with us. That trashy freak played us for fools." I wanted to call the police, but Sheila wouldn't hear of it.

"She's had a hard life," she said quietly. Of course Sheila's excuse only made me madder and I ranted about what I thought the girl needed. At one point I slammed my hand against the door so hard I thought I'd broken a bone. Between the pain and the frustration I started sobbing on the bed, my knees pulled tightly against my chest. "Now we're broke," I whimpered, "flat broke."

When Sheila sat next to me on the bed, I tried to pull away, but she touched my cheek softly and I let her stroke my hair. "Everything will be okay," she whispered. "I've still got twenty dollars in my purse." I heard her fiddling with her wallet. "Look," she said, holding the bill. I rolled over and groaned.

Then the damnedest thing happened. With my face red, wet and tight from crying, I watched her pull from the night stand a green-colored Gideon's Bible. She set the book carefully on her knee, as though getting ready to give a good long reading. Her hand hovered along the edge, then flipped the book open at random. And there, nestled flat against the spine, was a hundred dollar bill.

After coffee and pancakes, we topped the gas tank and set out again. We drove through Flagstaff, then, just past Williams, took a detour to visit the Grand Canyon. I wished then that I had remembered to bring my camera, which was in my trailer in Bakersfield, though if I had, that damned Chiquita probably would have lifted it, too. But even with my bad blood for Chiquita, looking down into the mighty canyon made me feel as though the all chasing around we were doing was silly: God was everywhere, in everything we saw. At the time I supposed that sentiment must have been childish and simplistic, but I remember it comforted me and even served to soften my heart toward Chiquita. Sheila didn't mention it, but I felt that she knew what I was thinking and was glad, too.

By the time we got to Tuba City, at the junction to Noxema, it was already dark, so we pulled over for the night at a little motel with tiny cabins set in a semi-circle. Already we were running low on money, and I was beginning to worry. "Have faith," Sheila said, so I drew a few breaths of desert air and did my best to follow her advice. And that night, in contrast to the tortured night before, I had a peaceful sleep and a lovely dream.

I was a child again, six or seven years old, playing with my mother in an immense field of yellow flowers. None of this was like the childhood I remember; for, in fact, I'd been raised by an older couple who adopted me after my mother died from a massive hemorrhage after giving birth. My father, a soldier overseas, had died in a freak accident three months before I was born. Or at least that was the story. In the dream my mother wore a long blue dress the color of the sky. We both laughed as she chased me through the tall stalks, and when she finally caught me we tumbled together and rolled among the flowers, laughing in each other's arms. I felt the grass against my cheek, smelled the blossoms, the earth. My mother brushed my hair back from my face and when I looked at her she was smiling down at me. I couldn't help thinking she was the most beautiful woman in the world. It was all so tender and it made me feel so incredibly full and tight in the chest that I woke myself whimpering. And as I opened my eyes in the gray twilight, I felt overwhelmed by melancholy, yet happier than I'd felt in a long time.

For several minutes I lay in bed, my eyes closed, the covers drawn tightly around me, trying to recapture the dream. Only when I heard the faint jingle of wind chimes did I re-open my eyes. Then, as I grew accustomed to the half-light, my gaze wandered. I saw that the bed next to mine was already remade; Sheila was not in the room. Softly I called out as I slipped my covers, but there was no answer. She wasn't in the bathroom. Finally, wrapping a sweater around my shoulders, I moved to the window and parted the curtains.

Directly outside, someone had suspended cylindrical aluminum chimes from the eaves of the porch. In the distance beyond, near the center of the gravel parking lot, I saw three deer gathered around Sheila. I watched as she fed them something from her palm and stroked their heads. In the quiet dawn, I heard my heartbeat, then the chimes and Sheila's clear voice singing. I listened for several minutes until something—the noise of a car coming up the road, perhaps—startled the deer and they bounded off, disappearing behind the nearest cabin.

When Sheila started back toward the room, she was still singing. In her hand she held a single rose. I busied myself getting dressed. "Those deer are hungry," she said, shutting the door. "I fed them some tortilla chips." I stared into my cosmetic bag. There was no shower in the room, no hot water. I decided not to wear any makeup.

Outside, the cool air was still and I could feel the barren desert all around us. We threw our luggage into the car and set out for Noxema, a three hour drive. In a diner there we asked a waitress about Albert Newton. The woman pulled back on her heels and narrowed her eyes: "He's that nut out in the desert," she said, as though she were accusing us of a crime. "He's not from around here, you know," she added. Clearly she wasn't much interested in helping us find him, so we let it drop and pushed our mugs forward for a refill.

On our way out the door, we met an Arizona State Trooper heading inside for breakfast. "Excuse me, officer," Sheila said, "Can you give us directions to Albert Newton's Starlight Ministry? We saw him on television last week and we're here on vacation." The trooper, a big middle-aged man, hooked a thumb in his wide black gun belt and stared at us from behind his sunglasses. He looked down at his feet and tapped the dust from one boot with the toe of the other.

"I'll give you ladies some advice," he said. "If I were you, I'd forget about Newton and go visit the National Parks. Arizona's a beautiful state and it's a pity it attracts trash like Newton." Sheila tried to interrupt him, but he raised his hand. "It's a free country and all we've got on him so far is rumor and hearsay, so if you're still interested, drive down the street a couple of blocks till you see a clapboard church. Next door you'll see a house with an office where you can get more information than a sane person would want about the 'Starlight Ministry.'"

"Thank you so much, officer," Sheila said.

"Is Newton some kind of criminal?" I cut in.

"Well, Ma'am, so far we can't say for sure that he's breaking any laws, but there's been talk of brainwashing and illegal drugs, and one woman told the newspaper in Flagstaff that there's wild sex going on, too." He blushed behind his sunglasses. "Excuse me for being candid." I nodded my head and was about to ask something else when he touched his hand to his hat and moved toward the door. "Morning now. You ladies be careful and enjoy Arizona."

We followed the officer's directions to the church, which, as it turned out, was impossible to miss, for the box-like old structure had been transformed into a mural depicting the desert, mountains and sky. The lower portions of the painting showed the buildings of a tiny town over which hovered a number of large cigar-shaped silver space ships. Above this scene the steeple tower loomed large with the smiling portrait, displayed on all four sides, of a man we later learned was Jesus Christ the Alien, a.k.a. Albert Newton.

After parking the car in front of a ramshackle bungalow next to the church, we walked up the flag-stone pathway to the door. Loud, bizarre flute music emanated from within. I pounded on the door. Half a minute later the music ceased and a woman with frizzy hair and wild eyes appeared. Her neck was bent from the weight of many pairs of colored wooden beads, her face wrinkled and deeply tanned from constant expo-sure to the sun. She studied us and rubbed her eyes as though we'd awakened her. "Hello," she said, finally, in a voice hardly louder than a whisper. "Welcome to the Starlight Ministry."

She ushered us into what passed for an office. The room was crowded with a metal desk piled high with papers, a four drawer filing cabinet, two phones, and a couch covered with a Navaho blanket. A combination of travel posters from various area National Parks—Brice and Zion Canyons, the Painted Desert, Arches and the Grand Canyon—and framed photographs of

U.F.Os decorated the walls. Stacked boxes of printed brochures and pamphlets bulged in the corners. "I'm Raya," the woman said, offering us a warm, dry palm,"can I get you some herb tea?"

When we told her why we were there, she seemed relieved. "For a second I thought you might be from the newspapers," she told us. "We've had so much attention since the television show. I'm not very good at handling publicity, so it was terrible being stuck here while that was going on."

"Stuck here?" Sheila said.

Raya explained that each of the members of the commune took turns manning the office in shifts while the others continued to live in the desert. "I hate being here," she said. "The sick weight of civilization presses in on you. Anything that's not tribal contributes to the sickness. But I suppose someone must be here to get the mail. And, of course, to greet lovely seekers like you," she added, smiling.

When Sheila asked about the church, Raya told us that the ministry had bought the property, along with the house we were in, several years earlier, with the intention of holding weekly services. The townspeople, however, had other ideas. "They directed so many bad vibes and so much negative energy at us that we had to give it up after a few months. Most people are lost, you know. They go around with their eyes closed. Of course it hurts a little at first when you open yourself to the light. Then suddenly, after you've adjusted to the shock of rebirth, you can see all the beauty around you."

Sheila nodded politely. I wanted to know about the space ships on the mural. "What's all that about?" I asked.

Raya reached into one of the boxes behind her and handed me a staple-bound booklet. "In this publication you'll find a concise summary of our beliefs," she said in a husky whisper. Sheila and I leaned closer. "It doesn't take long to read and it will change your life. All we ask is a five dollar donation to help cover our printing expenses."

"Can we visit the commune?" Sheila asked. "Does Albert Newton preach there?"

"Yes, of course," said Raya, "you may visit for as long as you like and partake of the rituals and soul-healing practiced by our spiritual leader. But first, read the book."

"How do we get there?"

"It's all in the book." Sheila opened her purse and pulled out the last of our money. She handed Raya five of the six remaining singles.

"Can you draw us a map or something?" I asked.

"It's in the book."

I sighed loudly and Sheila smiled at Raya, who smiled back. Then we both thanked Raya for her time and left with Sheila clutching the pamphlet to her breast. I saw that the map was printed on the back cover. Though there was only a quarter tank of gas left in the car, I left town without bothering to spend our last dollar. As we headed into the baking desert, Sheila read the booklet aloud from beginning to end. It was a long, dull drive and it helped to have something to listen to along the way.

The pamphlet began with a personal history of the Alien Messiah, who'd first appeared as a baby somewhere in New Jersey some forty-six years earlier. After a childhood in which his only miracle had been a stand-out performance as a little-league pitcher, Albert Newton briefly attended junior college, received an early honorable discharge from the army due to chronic medical problems, married his high school sweetheart, and took a job in Erie, PA, selling life insurance. At the age of twenty-six, however, something happened which would, according to the author of the booklet, "alter the course of human consciousness."

While walking his dog through the star-lit streets of Erie one summer night, Albert Newton had been "abducted" by aliens from another galaxy and taken aboard their space ship. "In the simplistic mythology of traditional Christians, these aliens were what might be termed 'angels,'" Sheila read, "for they, in fact, exist only to serve God." All of this and much more was revealed to Albert by means of a truth chamber aboard the space ship. It was a kind of walk-in closet in which huge amounts of information could be absorbed rapidly into the brain. When the former insurance salesman emerged from the chamber and was transported back to his corner of the Quaker state, no time appeared to have lapsed. I'd guess his dog was just as he left it, still squatting over the wet grass the way they do, straining to finish his business.

Someone strolling by probably wouldn't have noticed anything unusual happening in the neighborhood, even though, according to the booklet, "humanity had been forever transformed; for Albert Newton was now resolute in the knowledge that he was no ordinary human, but rather a spiritually advanced being—one of the many 'suns' which God had sent into the universe to spread his light and truth. That Albert had been deposited in an pre-embryonic state years earlier and had been allowed to be born and raised as though he were truly of this planet and this species was a part of God's great plan for spiritual renewal. Albert himself had undergone this remarkable change. Flesh and blood, he was both God and man."

Soon after what the author called the "Great Revelation," Newton ditched his wife and dog, quit the insurance business, and began the Starlight Ministry in an abandoned factory on the shore of Lake Erie. He soon attracted his first followers, a bunch of high school kids. As a result of a police raid and trumped up charges of pornography and moral indecency—which were never proven, and which, according to the pamphlet, Albert had calmly prophesied—the ministry headed west to "The Chosen Country," an old Arizona homestead one of his groupies had inherited. "Now ministry members live in perfect harmony with nature, themselves and God. In this country of vast expanses, star-filled night skies, and on-going practice of tribal ritual, the community thrives to this day, attracting dozens of new members each year, and sending hundreds of visitors back into the world to spread the gospel of Jesus Christ Alien." Sheila stopped reading and closed the booklet.

"We should be getting close to the turn-off," she said. "We'd better concentrate on the landmarks." I nodded, wishing we'd have thought to bring along something to drink. Ahead of us on the highway, heat rose, blurring the road into a mirage of water. The dry

69

air from the open windows blew our hair into our faces as we sped along. Twenty minutes later we approached a huge outcropping of stone that may or may not have resembled a face seen in profile. "I think that's it," said Sheila. I wasn't so sure. If we misinterpreted the landmarks, we might find ourselves lost once we left the road, for there were many dirt tracks leading off the highway and into the desert. I pulled to the side of the road so we could take a closer look.

"It's supposed to look like Albert Newton," I said, as we stared at the rocky tower.

"Use your imagination," suggested Sheila. I stared at the rocks a long time, but no matter how hard I tried, I couldn't find a face there. Finally, I gave up.

"Look, Sheila, I can't see anything. But if you say there's a face, then I guess this has got to be it." I wiped the back of my sweaty neck with my palm. Sheila nodded as I guided the car back onto the highway. We clocked the next three miles on the odometer, and sure enough, just as the final tenth of a mile registered, we came to a junction from which a dirt road led out from the highway and into the desert.

I swung the car off the pavement and onto the hard-packed dirt of the desert floor. A cloud of dust spun up behind us. Though unpaved, the road was wide, as though it had been graded to accommodate heavy traffic. Almost immediately after leaving the highway, we began a gradual climb. Then, about half a mile further, the road made a sharp curve, followed by a dip. As we came up out of the trench, we could see, several hundred yards in the distance, a towering jumble of bleached lumber against the flat sky. "What on earth?" I said.

Sheila shook her head. "It looks like those dinosaur bones you see in a museum." As we drew closer I realized that we were looking at the skeletal remains of an abandoned roller coaster. Closer still, we saw an old Merry-Go-Round, its carved horses and circus animals smashed under the wreckage of the turreted roof.

"Who would build an amusement park in the middle of nowhere?" I asked. Again, Sheila shook her head. I stopped the car and we both stared at the rotting trestles. I tried to imagine screaming riders careening down the steep tracks and slamming through the tight turns, calliope music and the bobbing motion of the carousel. "This is madness," I said. We drove on.

Above the ruins, the road was in much poorer condition, full of ruts and boulders, so I slowed the car. After a few miles, the dirt road turned into a jeep trail of parallel tire tracks. Sheila unbuttoned her blouse and fanned her chest with the Starlight Ministry booklet. Ahead of us a sidewinder slid out from the sagebrush then popped beneath the tires. The sound made me shudder. My mouth tasted faintly of iron as I watched the needle on the gas gauge edge toward empty. A glowing peach pit sprouted in my stomach, another in my throat, as we crossed the long shadows of mesas rising high off the desert floor. My mind spun a movie about a family in a covered wagon with broken wheels and dead oxen. Somewhere nearby I could sense bones bleaching in the sun. Doom seemed to dwell in the barren hills around us. Just for the hell of it I switched on the radio and let the static fill the air as I searched the dial for something familiar.

As the rocks and ruts beat up the car beneath us, we climbed steadily through a moonscape of pink and tan sandstone. Stopping for a moment at the top of a rise, we got out and surveyed the land. Emptiness and desolation spread to the horizon in every direction, broken only by the long trail of dust from our tires that still hung in the air miles below. A dizzy stillness pressed in on us. Without a word, we got back into the car and drove on. Several miles later the engine coughed twice, then sputtered. "Oh God, no," I said. Then it died. I rested my head against my forearms on the steering wheel as we coasted to a stop.

When I opened my eyes again, I checked the odometer. We'd traveled thirty-six miles since we left the highway. In a few hours it would be dark. We had no food, no water. I could barely swallow and my tear ducts were too dry for crying. "This is it," my brain kept screaming, "this is it!" Then Sheila grabbed the keys out of the ignition and opened the trunk. She came back with a scarf wrapped over her head and our coats piled in her arms. "You'd better change into some jeans and put on walking shoes," she called out. But I couldn't move. I felt my head slip back down against the steering wheel. Sheila opened the door for me and tugged at my arm. "Don't worry, Mary" she said, "it's only a little bit further." I shook my arm free and jumped out of the car. I wanted desperately to uncoil myself, strike out, bite her in the face.

After I'd changed my clothes, I picked my coat up off the hood where Sheila had left it and walked up the trail to where she was squatting in the dust behind the lacy shadow of a tumbleweed. "Maybe we should go back the way we came. At least we know how far it is to the highway," I said.

"Don't be silly," Sheila smiled through cracked lips. "Come on." She stood up and began walking. There was nothing I could do but follow her up the jeep trail. We must have walked for hours. In time the sun began to slide lower in the sky and a late afternoon breeze rustled the sagebrush. Suddenly I became aware of a presence, as though someone or something were watching us. I picked up a rock and held it in my hand as we descended a short grade. To the side I glimpsed a quick movement. Then I focused in on them: coyotes. They were shadowing us in the distance.

"Now we've had it," I told Sheila. "Soon it will be dark, and we won't be able to see the path ahead of us. We have no way of making a fire or weapons and they'll smell our fear and move in on us when we're too sleepy and weak to do anything about it. They'll tear us to pieces. There's a whole pack of them. We're going to die out here!"

"No we aren't, Mary. The coyotes will leave us alone. They're cowards. As long as they can see us moving or they can hear our voices, they'll keep their distance." Then Sheila began to sing a strange kind of song with words I couldn't understand. The coyotes pricked their ears, then trotted along with us again as we walked. "It's Latin," she told me, though I hadn't asked.

It was almost completely dark and I was nearly delirious from dehydration and fatigue, when we spotted a fire in the distance. Below us, in a narrow valley bordered by sheer red rock walls, I could barely make out signs of civilization: the tiny shapes of cars and trucks, some low buildings outlined against the far cliffs. "Look!" I yelled, then took off running. Several hundred yards later I doubled over on the ground, my stomach knotted with cramps. Sheila stroked my hair as I fought for breath. Through the darkness I thought I saw the red eyes of the coyotes.

It must have taken us another hour to reach the Starlight Commune. I was so weak that I had to throw my arm around Sheila's neck and lean my weight against her part of the way. At times my legs barely functioned. When we finally crossed the last of the ridges along the valley floor and headed into the commune, the first person we saw was a man dressed in a loin-cloth and a leather vest, who was sitting on his haunches smoking a pipe. His long hair and beard were braided with knots and beads. He stared at us in disbelief as we hobbled toward him. Finally he stood up and approached us. If he talked at all I don't remember what he said. He led us into a large building made of stone and wood, which I would later learn was a communal eating and sleeping hall.

Inside, some forty or fifty people were sitting cross-legged on the ground in a large circle around a fire, eating with their fingers out of wooden bowls. Though most were dressed in carefully fashioned rags, many of the men and some of the women, as well, were naked to the waist and the reflection from the fire splashed orange light over their skin. When Sheila let go of me I collapsed on the floor. Someone pressed a bowl of water to my lips.

In the morning we were given cold porridge and a large hunk of dark bread. Then we were introduced to the children and the other women. One, a pretty blond girl of twenty named Sunshine, informed us that she would be our guide for as long as we chose to stay. The men, she told us, had already gone off to work the fields or hunt.

We spent the day with Sunshine, touring the community. She showed us the corn and bean fields, the wells and windmills, and the school and play areas for the children, as well as the communal kitchen and ritual bath facilities. Finally, she led us up a steep path to the top of a mesa, a sacred place at which they'd somehow constructed a circular enclosure of huge boulders. This, Sunshine told us, was where they held their religious festivals, their prayer and meditation sessions. From a mesa high above the barren desert, the Alien Christ preached his Holy Word.

The three of us stood together near the edge of the cliff and surveyed in silence the vast emptiness beyond. "Where is Albert Newton?" Sheila finally said, her voice barely louder than a whisper. Sunshine led us to a flat rock, where we sat and listened as she told us about Newton's habits of fasting and meditating alone in the desert. She explained how he lived without food, water or human company, "sleeping under the blanket of the universe, communing with his Father above." A dreamy, drugged tone crept into her voice as she lectured us about the divine qualities of Albert Newton, former life insurance salesman from Erie, PA.

When Sunshine finally stopped babbling, Sheila took the opportunity to ask when we might actually meet Albert Newton. "Is he going to preach anytime soon?"

"Oh yes," said Sunshine, "he directs our communal worship once a week. And he presides as well at our ritual cleansing ceremonies. The best time to meet him is then. If you want, you can come tonight. We all do it together. The Messiah says it's the best way to get to know God."

"We'll be happy to attend," said Sheila.

The "ritual cleansing" took place every Monday, Wednesday and Friday evening at eight o'clock. All adult members of community were expected to participate, as well as any consenting guests. Menstruating women were prohibited from attending and stayed in the lodge to supervise the children, while the rest of the community gathered, by the divine grace of the Alien Christ, in the large, tightly sealed stone structure which served as a sauna and bath house. The building, I remembered from our tour, was divided into three rooms of roughly equal size. One room contained wooden benches and a cast iron stove sunk halfway into a pit in the center of the floor and fitted with a welded rack to hold the stones which produced the steam. The second room held a large redwood tub filled with cold water from a nearby rainwater storage tank. The third room was a large open space with a fireplace at one end and grass mats, futons and throw pillows on the floor.

After dinner that night, each participant was served a bowl of murky fermented mash, which, in addition to its high alcohol content, also contained, we learned afterwards, a potent if not downright toxic blend of natural hallucinogenics in the form of peyote and magic mushrooms. As soon as we had consumed this vile-tasting beverage, Sunshine led us outside, where groups of people stood in small clusters, some holding hands in a circle, or else pressing their palms to each other's chests, as they stared silently at the night sky. "Look up at the sky," she whispered to us, "and find your meditation star." I tilted my head back and closed my eyes. "Now Mary, put your hand against my heart while I put mine against Sheila's and she puts hers against yours." I opened my eyes as she took my hand and pressed it to her bosom. Then she guided Sheila's hand to mine. "Press my hand to your flesh," she told Sheila. "Feel how our hearts beat together as though they are one. Feel yourself in harmony with the universe," she recited, breathlessly. Above us the stars seemed to be spinning wild and random patterns.

We stood staring at the heavens together for a long time in the cool desert night. The blood seemed to be draining slowly from my head. My mouth felt dry and I was getting dizzy. Nearby I heard a body fall heavily to the ground, then another. A moment later my knees buckled beneath me and I collapsed onto the hard-packed earth. This seemed to signal an end to the star-gazing phase of the ritual, for as Sheila and Sunshine helped me quickly to my feet, I could see that the others were now making their way across the dark field toward the brightly-lit bathhouse. The three of us stumbled after them.

Inside, the large room was already stiflingly hot and humid. I sat down on one of the benches near the door and watched as people shed their clothes be-neath the warm glow of kerosene lanterns. In front of me Sunshine pulled her loose cotton blouse over her head, revealing her freckled chest and breasts, then kicked off her sandals and stepped out of her long skirt. She pushed her clothes into a pile against the wall beneath the bench and motioned for us to do the same. As I struggled to my feet, I could feel the sweat which had already formed beneath my arms begin to roll down my sides.

I looked over at Sheila and saw that she was already unbuttoning her blouse. Suddenly I began to laugh. Around me others started as well, pulled into the web of my hysteria. I covered my face with both hands. I couldn't stop. Finally, I began undressing. When I was completely naked I kicked my clothes into a pile and, still laughing, sat back down on the bench with my legs crossed and my arms folded over my breasts. I watched as a tall, thin man took a ladle from a wooden bucket and moved toward the stove. His penis slapped against his thigh as he walked. He poured the water over the stones, which hissed loudly and produced a geyser of steam.

Then a squat, semi-balding man wearing only sunglasses stood near the center of the room, spread his arms wide, and began chanting in an unintelligible language. His thick neck, chest, back and thighs were covered with a pelt of dark body hair, giving him a troll-like appearance. Immediately, a woman approached with a lighted candle, which she offered to him. He held the flame aloft in both hands, as she stood opposite him and joined his song. Sunshine, who was sitting next to me on the bench, leaned close. "It's him," she whispered. Soon two others, a man and a woman, stood and added their voices to the chant, which built slowly in intensity, as two by two, the community rose to join in. Transfixed, I stared at the candle as the voices grew louder and louder around me. Then a man across the room stood and I felt Sheila's naked thigh brush against my own as she rose to her feet.

I could hear Sheila clearly above the others. Full and melodic, her voice expanded to fill the room with the same hymn she'd sung as we wandered through the desert the evening before. I stared at her with wide eyes, gasping and trembling: Her large, pear-shaped breasts swayed with each new breath. Her belly, arching round and graceful, swelled huge above her hips, the skin taut with new life. Miraculously, Sheila was pregnant.

As suddenly as it had begun, the chanting ended and some of the singers began moving into the adjacent bath room. I could hear the sound of water as their bodies slipped into the cool tub. Elsewhere in the room couples embraced and kissed. Close by I saw a woman close her fist, and then her lips, around a man's erect penis as another man rubbed against her from behind. I stood up and watched as Sheila crossed the room and headed through the steam toward Albert Newton. She paused before him and as she spoke he reached his hand toward her and touched her swollen belly. Then he placed both hands on it and rubbed lightly in a circular motion as they talked.

As I watched them, I suddenly felt hands moving over my own belly, followed by warm breath at my ear. Soft lips caressed my neck, and teeth nipped at my ear lobe. I felt the hot, rigid flesh of an erection press against my buttocks as hands cupped my breasts, fingers pinched and rolled my nipples. Yet even as the hands glided along my thighs, even as they slid into the wetness between my legs, my eyes never left Sheila. I saw Newton slip an arm around her waist and guide her toward a bench, then watched as he dressed her in a white robe. As I spread myself upon the floor, I saw him kneel before her and place sandals carefully on her feet. I stiffened, then moaned as he led her to the exit. With my hands grasping tightly behind my knees, I thrust my pelvis and climaxed as the door closed behind her.

When I opened my eyes, Albert Newton was standing above me, smiling and erect. He tapped my grunting partner on the shoulder as if cutting in on a dance and the man immediately stopped his thrusting and disengaged. Newton hurried to take his place. His hands guided me into position as he rolled me onto my hands and knees and mounted me from behind. He leaned across my back and reached beneath me to caress my dangling breasts with one hand. The other hand tugged gently at my hair, pulling my head back so that my eyes rolled and my mouth opened wide.

I don't remember what happened next, though it's easy to imagine. In the morning I woke with a terrible headache. After staring blankly at the ceiling for several minutes, I realized that I was lying naked beneath a blanket, surrounded by dozens of other naked, sleeping bodies. I pushed myself up onto my knees and struggled to my feet. My bladder and head hurt and I was sore between the legs and nauseous. I stumbled into the deserted sauna room, found my clothes, and dressed, fumbling with the buttons on my blouse.

Hanging carefully onto the door for balance, I stepped out into the brilliant sun, where I found Sheila crouched on the ground next to the entrance, her back against the stone wall of the building. Sitting next to her, dressed in a black leather motorcycle jacket, tight pants and boots, and smoking a cigarette, was Chiquita. Immediately, Sheila sprang to her feet. When I saw that she was no longer pregnant, I fell to my knees and retched onto the barren earth.

After a while Sheila and Chiquita each hooked a hand under my arms and pulled me up. "We're leaving now," said Sheila. Tears welled up in my eyes as the vomit burned my throat. I spit some more bile onto the ground.

"How?" I managed to ask, but they were already dragging me up the path that led across the valley. We stopped behind an outcropping of rocks and Chiquita handed me a plastic water bottle.

"Rinse your mouth out with this," she said. "It will make you feel better."

"Then drink a little, but not too much," added Sheila.

When my mind and throat were clear enough that I could talk again, I asked Chiquita, "What are *you* doing here?"

She laughed and lit another cigarette with a disposable lighter. "I knew you'd say that," she said, blowing smoke at the clouds above. "Let's just put it this way: I saw on the map where you were going, so I followed you here on my bike."

"Your bike?" I stammered. The sunlight was making me dizzy. "But why? You stole our money."

"I didn't *steal* the money," Chiquita snorted, "I *borrowed* it. There's a difference. You pay back a loan and that's what I'm here to do." She unzipped one of the front pockets of her jacket, pulled out a rolled wad of cash, and handed it to me. "You even made some interest," she smiled. "Go ahead, count it."

I shook my head and handed the money to Sheila. "I can't deal with any of this right now," I said.

"Chiquita told me she won the money and a motor-cycle in a card game," Sheila explained. I rubbed my eyes and groaned. "And on the way here she found your car and put gas in it for us."

"I figured as long as I was heading into the desert by myself I'd better take along some extra fuel," Chiquita said, "so I strapped a five gallon can to the sissy bar with bungee cords."

"You should have been a Boy Scout," I said, then leaned over and retched again.

As soon as I felt well enough to continue, we walked on. After several miles we left the path, scrambling down a steep embankment and into a narrow canyon. "It's a short cut," said Chiquita. We moved through the canyon until we arrived at a secluded area where a few green plants and even some small trees grew. "There's a spring here," Chiquita told us. She led us to a small pool of water. "I saw smoke coming from here yesterday afternoon and figured this might be where you were. So I left my bike up above and came down to take a look. When I got here all I found was some weird-looking naked guy in sunglasses sitting around drinking beer, eating Twinkies and jerking off. After a while he left, so I thought I might as well help myself to one of his beers. That's when I discovered the cave." We followed close behind as she pushed forward through the brush and shrubs behind the pool, uncovering the entrance to a hidden cave. "Wow!" Chiquita said, pointing to the yellow flowers of a wild climbing rose bush that partially blocked the dark and narrow opening, "that wasn't blooming yesterday."

Inside the cave we found an old mattress, a stack of pornographic magazines, several cases of beer, a large stock of canned and dried food, a few fire-blackened pots, matches, and newspapers. Half concealed at the back of the cavern was a small motorcycle with knobby tires, and in the fire pit near the entrance were the partially burned remains of tin foil and cigarette filters. "I suppose this is where Albert Newton lives," said Sheila, matter-of-factly.

After leaving the cave, we continued up the canyon several hundred yards, following a foot path that eventually led back to the jeep trail that ran along the ridge above. Once there, Chiquita retrieved her motorcycle from where she had hidden it behind a pile of boulders several hundred feet from the road. The bike was a massive Harley Davidson, gleaming with chrome. As Sheila and I stood to the side watching, Chiquita straddled the wide seat and reached for the choke valve. Then she unfolded the kick starter and jumped her weight against it. As the engine turned over, caught and roared to life, the throaty popping of exhaust exploded in the desert air, echoing down the canyon we'd just traversed.

Chiquita slid herself halfway onto the gas tank and called for us to get on the bike. I watched as Sheila placed her hands on the bald girl's shoulders and stepped over the seat. Then I squeezed myself into the tiny space left between her and the chrome sissy bar. As Chiquita slapped the bike into gear, hand-fed the gas, and eased out the clutch, the big back tire spun on the hard dirt, then suddenly grabbed traction, sliding the bike in a fishtail pattern and pelting the area behind us with pebbles and loose dirt. Her feet down for balance, Chiquita brought us slowly up to the road.

When we got to my car, she shut down the Harley and helped us prime the engine with gas from the can she'd left on the ground near the rear tire. I prayed behind the wheel as the engine cranked and cranked until the battery clicked and the starter froze. "Shit!" yelled Chiquita, "I must have flooded the fucker with all that gas." With the back of my hand I wiped the sweat from my brow and watched as she unzipped her leather jacket. "Jesus, it's hot out here," she said, pulling her arms loose and throwing it to the ground. Naked to the waist now, I could see the tattoos that covered her upper body. A colorful dragon stretched along her chest, its tail curling into the valley between her immense breasts, which were themselves decorated with spider webs spreading out from the nipples. Along her stomach, in large red and black block letters, were the words GOD IS LOVE. Suddenly I felt faint and rested my head against the steering wheel.

"Put your foot on the gas pedal and keep it to the floor," Chiquita called out. I could hear her blowing into the carburetor. A few minutes later she told me to give the ignition a try. "Come on, honey," she pleaded, "fire up, you bitch!" When the engine finally caught and started, we all gave out a cheer. Sheila got into the car with me as Chiquita put her jacket back on and straddled the Harley. I backed the car up and turned it around. Then we all took off, with Chiquita in the lead.

For a long time Sheila and I drove in silence, suffering from the mid-day heat and eating the dust from the motorcycle. Nevertheless, I was glad to be leaving this place with my body, mind and soul more or less still intact.

When we finally reached the highway again, Chiquita hopped off her bike and waved us to a stop. I killed the motor, and the three of us stood together in the sunlight. "Everything okay?" Chiquita asked.

"We're fine," said Sheila.

Chiquita shuffled her feet and kicked at a rock with the toe of her boot. "I'm going back to Vegas," she said, "got a little unfinished business to take care of there. You still planning to head east?"

"Arkansas," said Sheila.

"Right. Well, then, I guess this is good-bye." Chiquita embraced Sheila. "Good luck, Mary," she said, softly.

"Bless you." Sheila kissed her brow. They smiled at each other. Then Chiquita held out her arms to me. We embraced.

"Adios, Mary," she told me. "Take care of yourself." She slapped my back. "Make sure she gets plenty of rest," she said to Sheila, winking, "and no more substance abuse." Then she returned to her motorcycle, straddled the seat, and fired up the engine. We watched her put the bike into gear and ease out the clutch. She pulled onto the highway, then turned to wave over her shoulder. Sheila and I waved back, then stood together along the roadside and watched her disappear.

When we got back into the car Sheila took the wheel and drove to Albuquerque. I slept most of the way in a fitful stupor in which I endured visions of spiders crawling up my arms, heard choruses of trumpets, and imagined the trucks that passed us were stampeding hooves. By the time we checked into a motel that night, I was raging with fever and delirious. Sheila wrapped her coat around me and dragged me up an exposed stairway to our room, then undressed me and put me into the bed, where she piled on extra blankets to counteract my chills.

For days I stayed in bed, sweating, moaning, thrashing around as I drifted in and out of anxious, fever-ridden sleep. Sheila sat close by me the whole time, stroking my hair and pressing a cool washcloth to my forehead. She left only to get medicine or bring food. She bought a hot plate on which she brewed me tea and broth, fed me aspirins and soda crackers, poured liquids into me. Finally the fever broke and she began reading to me from books she'd bought. Though I barely had strength enough to follow, her voice was soothing. Later, she brought out some cards and we played game after game of Hearts and Old Maid.

"Chiquita gave us her lucky deck," Sheila told me.

We stayed two more weeks in Albuquerque. When I was well enough to dress and leave the room, we took a walk, resting every few blocks in order to help rebuild my strength. As I grew stronger we visited the old town, went to see movies, ate in restaurants, and passed pleasant mornings in a nearby park, where we read the newspaper and fed the pigeons.

Once a group of children flocked around us and Sheila produced a sack of peppermint sticks from her purse, which she handed out to them, laughing. Then we followed them to a little open air amphitheater, where a thin man with dark hair and a handlebar mustache was setting up a miniature stage. Dressed in a shabby tuxedo with long tails, a battered top hat and white gloves, he sang funny foreign songs as he worked. When he finished with the stage, he began pulling puppets out of a wooden box. Around us the children were getting excited. "He comes here every Wednesday," a little girl told us.

Finally he disappeared behind the tiny theater. A moment later the curtain opened on a room where a mother was holding her baby. Moving the mother puppet so that it produced a rocking motion, the puppeteer made his voice high, and began singing a lullaby. Then another puppet—a man dressed in a black suit—burst into the room. "What's for dinner?" he growled.

"We haven't any money to buy food," said the wife.

"Then we'll cook up this baby and eat it!" the husband roared. Around us, the children in the audience gasped.

"Oh, no, please!" said the wife, clutching the baby more tightly to her breast. The puppeteer made crying noises for the child.

"Stop that infernal racket," yelled the villain, "it's giving me a headache. Make it stop or I'll throw the brat out the window!" He moved to the tiny window and opened it, as the baby continued wailing. "Now hand over the child," he said, turning back to his wife.

"Never!" she called out, stepping back from him.

Suddenly Sheila stood up, grabbed her purse and hurried out of the amphitheater. By the time I'd caught up with her, she was leaning heavily against the far wall of a covered picnic area near the swings, her face buried in her hands.

"What's wrong, Sheila?" I asked, "it's only a Punch and Judy show."

"I'm sorry," she said, still hiding her face. "It's going to rain and I wanted to find shelter." Just then the first few drops began to fall. Then a barrage of fat raindrops exploded on the ground all around us. In the distance we could hear the children screaming and laughing as they ran for cover. "It was a cruel show," said Sheila.

That evening while I was watching television in our room, Sheila took a ball of yarn and some needles from her purse and started knitting. Fascinated, I watched the movement of her hands, listened to the rhythmic clicking of the needles. "What are you making?" I asked.

"Just a little something that might come in handy some day," she said. Intrigued, I asked if she'd teach me how to knit, and the next day she took me to a store filled with colored yarn. We bought a set of large needles for me to practice with and some variegated yarn. Each day after that we'd go to the park and sit together on a bench beneath an old tree, our needles clicking. Though I looked for him the following Wednesday, there was no sign of the puppeteer or his little stage.

Finally, one day I woke to find Sheila packing. "It's time for us to leave now," she said. There was no reason to argue with her. I'd recovered my health, and felt strong again, even restless. So we got in the car, found the interstate, and drove east. In the seat next to me Sheila unfolded a road map and pointed to a yellow dot.

"Why Ohio?" I asked. "What about that fire and brimstone guy with the rattlesnakes in Arkansas? Are we just going to skip him?" For a moment Sheila remained silent, staring out the window without expression. I thought perhaps she hadn't heard my question and was about to ask again when she spoke.

"I know now," she said slowly, "what all this is about."

"All what?"

"Everything."

"Really?" I said, "Since when? Tell me." When Sheila didn't say anything, I searched her face for a clue. Her brow was slightly wrinkled and she seemed distracted, as though she were concentrating on something important and difficult to put into words. When she noticed I was staring at her, her lips turned upward and she chuckled.

"I'm sorry, Mary," she said, "I'm just trying to remember. I have so much to tell you and I want to get it right."

"It's okay," I told her, "take your time." I switched off the radio and listened to the sound of the engine and the tires on the pavement beneath us. After several minutes, Sheila cleared her throat:

"I'm not really sure how to begin, Mary. I suppose I should tell you everything that seems important. My

parents . . . my parents were good people." Sheila
paused, looked out the window for a moment, then
started again.

"I was raised the middle child among two brothers
and two sisters. My parents were uneducated folks who
worked hard and tried to make the best life they could.
When I was eight we moved from my grandfather's
farm in Wisconsin to Ohio after my father had a fight
with 'the old man,' as he called him. Though no one
ever spoke of it, I still remember being awakened by
men's voices yelling and fists pounding on the table-
top. Anyway, we left soon after that. My dad was a proud
man, you see, and even though he'd spent his whole
life working the land, he found a job running some
kind of machine and moved us all far away from his
father's farm. He hated our town life in Ohio, hated
working in that factory. But he never went back to the
farm, and he never spoke another word to his father.
I guess he started drinking to numb himself against the
life he thought he owed us.

"In Ohio we lived in a rented two-story house in a
working class neighborhood. My mother stayed at
home; there was nothing else for her to do. Though
she disapproved of my father's drinking, she kept
quiet. Like most women, she never thought to complain. Instead, she hoped that her children would

redeem her life. The only time I ever saw her ask for anything she wanted herself was when she begged my father to buy a television set. Somehow the glow of the picture tube and the images dancing in our darkened living room seemed to comfort her.

"Together my parents stumbled through a hard, dull life. The only glory came when my older brother played quarterback on the high school football team. For my part, I was an average student with normal tastes and interests. All in all, throughout most of my childhood, we were an unremarkable family.

"Then, when I was fourteen, I had a strange and wonderful dream that filled me with longing and frightened me at the same time. I dreamed an angel came and hovered above my bed, his wings outstretched. He touched my forehead with his cool hand, and when I sat up he pressed his finger to my lips. 'Listen carefully, Mary,' he said, 'you are going to have a baby.' I remember waking up then and lying in my bed with my heart pounding. When I got up and went to the window, I could feel the heat rising up from the earth.

"The morning after the dream I had my breakfast and walked to school as usual. But all around me everything had changed. It was early spring and for the first time I could see the new buds just starting to green the trees. Colors were brighter and the sound of my own voice clearer, more distinct. I could feel my heart pumping blood.

"After school I walked home with my friends as usual. We talked about the clothes we'd seen in magazines and compared the boys at school to famous singers and actors until, one by one, my friends turned off and I was walking the last few blocks alone. Then, for some reason, instead of going home, I passed the street where I lived and continued walking. I had no idea where I was headed.

"I came to a construction site, a place on what was then the outskirts of town, where carpenters were putting up the wooden frames of a housing project. Fascinated, for the rest of the afternoon I watched them working. Then I went home, helped make dinner, and did my schoolwork. The next day I returned to the construction site. I loved the sound of busy saws and the rapping hammer noise. But most of all I loved the way sunlight shone on the tanned and sweaty torsos of the men working among the roof beams.

"On the third day, one of the carpenters, a handsome man about forty, offered me a cold drink from his thermos. I was hot, so I accepted, thanking him. His name was Joe, he told me. He was the lead man, and he traveled from job to job with his crew of framers. When he asked me why I was there, I told him I didn't know. He looked at me strangely, then rubbed his chin.

After that Joe was kind and gentle, as though he knew something I didn't. Though I could hear him yelling at the other men, he spoke to me softly, almost whispering. The next day I brought an old sweatshirt to sit on and saved my lunch from school. I wasn't surprised when he sat beside me, nor was he when I offered him half my sandwich.

"We continued to meet every day. Sitting on my sweatshirt, I'd alternate between doing my homework and watching the builders. At home, no one asked where I'd been, though my mother began looking at me strangely. After a while, Joe and I started meeting at the building site when everyone else was asleep. He'd lead me by the hand around the project, explaining in detail how the houses were put together. One day, my friends followed me after school and soon all the kids knew about Joe. The girls in my gym class used to look at my skinny body in the shower and laugh. They told me Joe was too old to be my boyfriend. But I didn't care what they thought. 'Joe's a nice man,' I told them, 'and, anyway, he's not my boyfriend.'

"One night my father got up to use the bathroom

just as I was walking downstairs in my coat. 'Where the hell are you going, Mary?' he asked. When I told him, he yelled and slammed his fist against the wall. I ran back to my bedroom and closed the door. 'You're not to see that man again,' he called after me.

"Two months later, when I began showing, everyone thought they knew the father. By then the framing was completed and the only information my father got was that Joe had moved with his crew to another city. And though I swore that Joe and I had never so much as kissed, no one believed me, especially my father, who refused to speak to me. 'You've shamed me,' is all he would say.

"A month later I was removed from school and sent to a home for unwed mothers. In this depressing, cold place, locked away by themselves, pregnant girls waited to give birth to unwanted children. The counselor told me that my parents had already signed the papers authorizing that my baby be placed immediately for adoption. Though this knowledge was meant to comfort and relieve me, instead it caused me terrible pain. The thought of losing my baby made me crazy, and I began dreaming up ways to escape. Though I had no money and nothing of any value to sell, I ran off in the middle of the night, seven months pregnant.

"The police picked me up a few hours later while I was begging for change at the bus station, and I spent the remainder of my pregnancy locked in a juvenile detention facility. As my due date grew closer I became more and more frantic: I couldn't bear losing my baby to adoption.

"Finally my labor arrived. The counselors, doctors and other adults had warned me about the pain. One even suggested childbirth would be a fitting punishment for me. 'Since you can't seem to keep your knees together, now you'll feel what it's like to be in the stirrups.' They tried to frighten me but it didn't work. Whenever I was alone, I'd lie on my bed with my hands spread over my belly and sing to my baby.

"Though I was terribly afraid when the contractions started, I wanted my baby badly. And I knew I'd done nothing wrong—even if people accused me, the child remained innocent. I tried barricading myself in my room. But when I didn't answer the roll call, they pushed their way in and took me to the hospital.

"The doctors were amazed that I didn't cry out. Instead, I smiled and told everyone how wonderful I felt. In truth, the labor was an intense pleasure unlike anything I'd ever felt; I knew then that it could never again be duplicated. 'She's hysterical,' I remember one of the nurses saying, as the baby's head crowned.

'I'm in ecstasy,' I told her, for the experience of pushing the baby through the birth canal was the most glorious moment of my life.

"When I saw my baby in the doctor's hands I reached out, but they pushed me down. The doctor cut the cord and I began screaming. I begged them to let me nurse my baby, pleaded with them to let me hold it, but they held me down and refused to answer my questions; I didn't even know what sex the baby was. Then, hiding behind a mask, the doctor injected me with a sedative.

'When I awoke, in the medical ward of the juvenile center, my womb was empty. I rolled out of bed and lay on the floor wailing until they came for me. I pounded them with my fists. I scratched at their eyes and bit them. They put me in a straightjacket. I don't know what happened after that."

Sheila stopped talking and sobbed. Her face was lined with pain. I'd never seen her express sorrow before. I was afraid to look at her, and I tried to concentrate on the highway ahead.

When Sheila began speaking again, her voice seemed different. It sounded hollow and muted, as though it had been blown a great distance through a narrow tunnel. "I returned to my family, to my school, to some of my friends, and no one ever brought up the subject of the baby," she said.

"In a small town like ours, an illegitimate child was scandalous. Wherever I went, I felt people's eyes on me and heard voices whispering. At home everyone except for my father tried to pretend nothing had happened. But it wasn't the same. I could feel their resentment, too.

"One day we went to a lake where my father liked to fish. He had a small aluminum boat that fit on the station wagon roof. He usually asked one of my brothers out with him while he fished, but that day he told me to sit in the boat. On the way out he pulled hard on the oars and didn't speak. After a while, when we were far from the shore, he stopped rowing, baited his hook and cast his line. For a long time he remained silent. He opened a beer and drank it as he stared at the water. Then he looked at me and said, 'Why did you have to shame me, girl? Each day I go to work knowing every man there thinks I've got a whore for a daughter.'

"I leaned forward and slapped him as hard as I could. 'I love my baby,' I told him.

"'You should be glad they took it from you,' he said, rubbing his face, 'else I'd have drowned the bastard.' He made me sit in the tiny boat for the rest of the afternoon while he fished and drank his beer in silence.

"I left home the next day—got on a bus and went as far away as possible, to California, where I found the kind of work I've been doing ever since. I've never seen my family again, though my sister writes at the holidays. She's married, has three kids. My parents are both gone, my oldest brother, too, killed in the war."

She paused again and looked at me. "I'm sorry," I thought to say, but she continued before I had the chance.

"Mary, I've never known a man intimately."

I pulled my gaze from the empty highway and looked at her. Her eyes were like a sky full of clouds. Why was she telling me this? I wondered.

"I don't have regrets," she continued, "though I'm sorry to have lived my life so alone."

"It's not too late," I began.

Sheila cut me off. "No, Mary, listen. That's not what I want to say. I'm trying to explain something I feel, something intuitive."

"About men?"

"About life. About everything. Men are part of it, though I'm hardly an expert. I want to talk about the differences. It's important, I think."

"Okay."

"They're inventive—men, I mean—always busy playing games of their own creation. You know as well as I do that most can't even drink a cup of coffee without describing their projects. But I believe men worship and fear women the same way they do the other mysteries of nature. They'd explain us away if they could, but they just don't understand. Their love is different than ours." Sheila paused for a moment and bit her lip. "I'm not making any sense," she said, sighing heavily.

"No, go on," I encouraged. I tried not to sound as confused as I felt.

Sheila bent her head. "Women bring life. Our hearts are sacred." She rubbed her palms together. "All this time I've lived alone, within myself, I never knew what happened to my baby. I've suffered a mother's grief." She turned to face me. "But now I know that the answer is in Ohio, in the place where I gave birth."

I didn't know what to say. Staring at the road ahead, I tried to remember what I could about the guests on the television show. None of them had been from Ohio. I couldn't find a connection.

"I'm going to get a copy of the birth certificate. It will tell me what I need to know," Sheila said. A glow like sunlight emanated from her. It surrounded her head. I wondered if it was possible for air to be so charged that static electricity became visible.

Then a shock sparked my brain, sending current through my body. The light around Sheila was something I remembered from my dream of the field with the yellow flowers. It was Sheila's face I'd seen staring down at me. From that moment I knew in my heart what my rational mind could not accept.

A long silence settled over us. Finally, as we entered Amarillo, Sheila pulled out the map again and unfolded it in her lap. "Would you mind if we took a side trip to New Orleans? she asked. "I've always wanted to go there."

She was stalling for time. Neither of us was in a hurry to reach Ohio. Perhaps we both knew. Or perhaps we were afraid that what we suspected wasn't really true. Looking back, I can't say exactly what I felt or believed.

By chance we arrived in New Orleans the morning of Mardi Gras. Though not yet noon, the downtown streets were crowded with traffic, the sidewalks full of people in wild costumes. Everywhere we went people seemed to be in an uproar. They were floating on their own expectation of a good time, drunk on the air around them. At hotel after hotel, clerks in sequined and feathered masks laughed when we asked for a room. In the lobby of a downtown high-rise, two men dressed as jesters took Sheila and me in their arms and danced with us. I heard Sheila laughing, and I started laughing, too, as we spun around the lobby, cheek to cheek with our partners. When we'd finished, the men directed us uptown, where they said our chances of finding a room for the night would be better.

Exhausted, I asked Sheila to drive. We headed away from the river, around the bustling French Quarter, across a bridge and several sets of railroad tracks, ending up at last in a run down section of town. We stopped in front of a brick building with a small wrought iron hotel sign hanging above a narrow door. After all our trouble earlier, Sheila suggested we double park. "If you're not back in three minutes, I'll find a place to park and come inside," Sheila told me, as I stepped onto the sidewalk.

Inside, the building was dark and musty. At first I had trouble seeing anything, but after my eyes adjusted, I noticed an ancient black woman in a house coat asleep behind a polished wooden counter. There was no bell to ring, so instead I cleared my throat. "Afternoon, honey," the woman said, opening one eye and looking me over. "You lookin' for someone special?"

"A room?" I muttered.

"Ah," she said, nodding her head and frowning. "This here is a boarding house, so not many come for that. Mostly we got regular guests. You understand?" I nodded my head. "But I got a room if you want it. How long you gonna stay?"

"I'm not sure. There are two of us."

"Husband?"

"No, another woman. We're tourists, traveling together." I opened my purse and took out my wallet. "I'll pay for two nights in advance."

She studied me again, rubbing her chin all the while. "You here for Mardi Gras?"

"Yes," I said. "We just got into town."

"All that fuss," she mumbled to herself. Then she spoke to me: "Not much celebrating goin' on under this roof. Nothing but ol' folks livin' here, and they gotta have their quiet." She turned her back to me, reached inside the cupboard behind her for a long-handled brass key. Then she pivoted slowly and dropped it into my palm. "We lock the outside door at ten o'clock," she said.

Just then I heard Sheila come through the entryway. I turned and saw she was carrying our bags, one in each hand. Behind me the old woman suddenly scrambled out from the counter, ran toward Sheila and fell to her knees, her hands clasped in front of her. *"Bénissez-moi, Sainte Vierge,"* she said. I watched as Sheila set the bags down on the worn carpet and lightly touched the woman on the forehead.

"Je te bénis, mon enfant," she whispered. She helped the woman to her feet and guided her to the chair behind the counter. After Sheila leaned over and whispered something in her ear, the woman smiled and closed her eyes. A moment later she began to snore. Meanwhile Sheila had picked up her bag and started toward the stairs.

"What was that about?" I asked, as we reached our room.

"One must be especially kind to the elderly," Sheila answered. "Sometimes they become innocent again, almost like children."

Inside, I tossed the key onto the night stand and flopped on the lumpy bed. "There's no bathroom," I groaned.

"Down the hall," Sheila said. I closed my eyes and thought of cockroaches.

Late that afternoon we walked to the French Quarter, which we guessed was about three miles from our hotel. By then the old section was so crowded with foot traffic that there were few cars on any but the widest streets. The closer we came to the center, the stranger the people around us seemed: it was nearly dusk, and as the sun fell people's spirits were rising. After buying cheap paper masks and plastic beads in a shop, we turned down a narrow side street and entered the hysteria. Immediately I felt myself swept into the stream of bodies. When I turned around, Sheila was gone.

As we had arranged previously to meet back at the hotel just before ten o'clock if we became separated, I wandered around on my own for a while before heading back. I was still following Chiquita's advice to stay away from booze. In all, Carnival was a disappointment. Aside from a few people singing and dancing joyfully, most of what I saw seemed empty and staged. Maybe the whole holiday was just an excuse for people to drink and party behind a mask for a few hours. Though around me people were laughing and singing, dancing and kissing, I couldn't join in. The couples groping in the shadows I passed made me think not of love, but of guilt and shame. The darkness, the masks, the very idea of Lent, all seemed depressing, part of some conspiracy to push humans further from love. I shouldered my way through a wall of bodies, toward an open square, where I hoped there would be more room to breathe.

If anything, the square was more crowded than the alley I'd just come from. Yet the energy was different. I looked around; no one was dancing. Though a few drunks crumpled along the sidewalk sang deliriously to themselves, everyone else seemed to be talking in excited whispers, craning their necks, pointing up at the sky. Next to me I heard a woman say the word miracle. "What's going on here?" I asked a man and a woman who were standing together staring with expressions of amazement at the church across the square.

"You mean you didn't see it?" they said in unison.

"See what?"

"The apparition."

"What are you talking about? I just got here."

The woman took off her mask and let it drop. It fell spinning like a leaf to the ground. She brushed her hair back from her face and shook her head slowly. She seemed to be having trouble grasping her thoughts and when she did speak the words came very slowly. "It happened less than five minutes ago." Behind me more people were pushing their way into the square, drawn by the current of rumor. Voices crackled. Shouts rang out. A few people burst drunkenly into the square, yelling. The place was full of voo-doo magic: One spell had been broken and another was busily being cast.

"Exactly what happened?" I pleaded.

"A figure of a woman appeared to be hovering above the roof of the church over there," the man said, excitedly.

"The Virgin," the woman added.

"Virgin?"

"A thirty second mass hallucination above the church of Our Lady of the Sacred Heart," called out a man nearby, "Queen of the Mardi Gras!" He laughed—at least I think it was a laugh, though it sounded more like a pig squealing—as he pushed his way past us and disappeared into the crowd. By now the square had become a confusion of dazed witnesses and carnival drunks. I headed toward the far corner of the block, where a main street would take me away from the French Quarter and back toward our hotel.

It was a long walk through the wild streets and when I finally arrived, it was already ten minutes after ten. Sheila, the woman from the lobby, and half a dozen old-folks from the hotel were standing together on the sidewalk singing spirituals and clapping their hands as they waited for me. "I'm sorry I'm late," I said as I approached them.

"That's okay, honey," the wrinkled clerk rasped, throwing her arm around my shoulder, "we're just glad you made it back okay. No telling what might happen Mardi Gras night." Though I wanted desperately to tell Sheila about the miracle and to ask her where she'd disappeared to, the old people pressed around me smiling and touching my hair. One toothless man nodded and winked, another kissed me on the cheek. Finally, I told them I was exhausted and excused myself to go up to bed.

"Best get your rest," someone said.

"Amen," called out another.

The next morning someone knocked on our door. When I answered I found a tray with cups of steaming chicory coffee, a pitcher of warm milk and a platter piled high with freshly-baked baignets resting on the floor outside. Over breakfast Sheila and I decided to go back downtown. "I didn't get to see much last night," Sheila told me. "After I lost you I came back to the hotel and played Gin Rummy and Hearts with the people here until it was time to lock up."

When we arrived back in the French Quarter it was mid-morning. The few shop-keepers who had opened their doors early all had the same thing on their mind: The Apparition. Everywhere we went people asked if we'd seen it. "I was there," a man selling junk jewelry from a stand on the corner boasted. "She was beautiful." Then he charged us seventy-five cents for a postcard of the square where the miracle occurred. Later, we saw a crowd of several hundred faithful had gathered to await another appearance. We stopped and looked at the church. "What do you think," a woman asked Sheila, "it's a miracle, no?"

"Oh, yes," Sheila said, politely, "what else could you call it?"

Later Sheila wanted to take a guided tour of an old mansion that had been turned into a museum. I was already tired of sight-seeing and told her I'd rather sit in the park and wait. For a while I was content to rest my feet, but after half an hour I got bored with watching the pigeons and began to look into the shop windows along the perimeter of the park. Then I turned down an alley and paused before the window of a shop specializing in tarot cards, voo-doo and the occult arts. The sign in the window read "open", but when I tried the door handle, it wouldn't budge. I put my face against the glass and saw a woman, her head wrapped in a blue patterned scarf, hurrying toward the door. She held her hand in front of her eyes. "Go away," she screamed, "too much light!"

We stayed in New Orleans exactly a week. On the fifth morning I woke up feeling sick, so I ran to the bathroom and threw up. "You're pregnant," Sheila said, after I'd come back from rinsing my mouth.

"I can't be," I told her. "My doctor told me years ago that I was infertile."

"Likelihood shouldn't be mistaken for truth," Sheila said. "Doctors don't know everything. Who can believe a science based on limited possibilities?" She smiled. "You missed your last period?"

"Yes," I said, wondering how she knew, "but that's

because I was so sick in Albuquerque. The fever and all." I sat down on the edge of the bed and looked at myself in the mirror.

"Oh, yes," Sheila said, "you're definitely pregnant. I can feel it. The energy of new life shines through you. You're lovely." She came toward me and kissed my forehead. Then she brought me her knitting bag. "These are for you," she smiled. In addition to the soft little blankets I'd seen her making over the past weeks, there were also several pairs of tiny booties, pink hats and dressing gowns. "I told you they'd come in handy," she said.

The following afternoon I fussed with one of those home pregnancy tests, which confirmed Sheila's diagnosis. It was impossible, yet it had happened. I didn't have any idea who the father was, and I didn't care. When I rushed out to tell Sheila the news, I found her asleep on the bed with her arms folded across her chest.

I was so excited that I had to tell someone, but when I ran downstairs the lobby was deserted. My hand shook as I shoved coins into the pay phone and dialed Fanny's number in Bakersfield. After three rings the answering machine clicked on. I waited for the beep, then screamed "I'm pregnant!" and hung up.

The next day we left for Ohio. As we drove through

a series of thundershowers, things began to get really weird. Sometimes I'd find Sheila sitting next to me in the car looking incredibly pale and as stiff and unblinking as a statue. Though her eyes were open she didn't seem to see, and when I talked to her, she didn't respond. I looked at her closely and she didn't appear to be breathing. When I reached out to touch her face, her cheek was as cold and smooth as marble. I let out a little cry. Suddenly she turned her head and smiled at me. An overwhelming scent of flowers filled the air. "Are you okay?" I asked, but she didn't answer.

Along route 55, just outside of Memphis, my car made a terrific thudding sound, then quit running. We coasted to the side of the highway and came to a stop opposite an immense field of red, yellow, and white flowers planted in neat, well-tilled rows. The soil around them was dark, rich and free of weeds. I'd never seen fields so carefully tended. In the distance a man was riding toward us on a tractor along a dirt road that ran parallel to the highway. As he drew closer, I could make out his bib overalls and baseball hat. By now Sheila and I had exited the car and were standing with the hood raised, silently inspecting the tubes and lumps of the engine compartment. As far as I could tell, nothing seemed broken.

Sheila shook her head and turned away from the

car. She stared at the approaching tractor and began waving her scarf in the air above her head. "Yoo-hoo," she called out. The farmer waved back from his seat, then parked on the road below us. He killed the engine, hopped off the tractor, waded an irrigation ditch, and began scrambling up the side of the hill. He was a lean man of about sixty, hardened from his work. His sharp face looked something like the claw end of a hammer. As he climbed, he wiped his hands on the legs of his overalls. "You ladies having car trouble?" he called out, staring hard all the while, first at me, then at Sheila.

For a moment he stood before us, still staring, his hands deep in his pockets. Then he did the most incredible thing. Right there, on the interstate, with cars speeding by us all around, he knelt in the mud and kissed Sheila's feet, then mine. When Sheila finally touched the back of his head, he rose up again. There were tears running down his cheeks. Without a word, he wiped his eyes on his sleeves and led us across the damp fields to his house. He stamped his feet hard on the porch to clean the mud off his boots, then held the door open and waved us forward. Inside, he pointed to a black telephone with one of those old style dials with the holes that spin inside the circle. We could hear him setting out dishes and working in the kitchen as we called for a tow truck.

The farmer asked us to make ourselves comfortable in the parlor, then, a few minutes later, led us to the kitchen, where he began setting the most wonderful food before us: freshly-baked bread, huge, uneven slabs of sunflower-colored butter, chicken roasted in herbs, baby onions and peas in white sauce, plates of fruits and cheeses. As we ate he continued working— slicing bread and meat, wrapping food in wax paper, brewing coffee. Finally, smiling shyly, he brought two big slices of apple pie and two steaming mugs of coffee with cream and set them on the table before us. Then he went back to the counter, folded the lip of a fat paper sack, and set it on the table as well. "This is for you, too…" He looked at the floor. "A person gets hungry traveling…" He stood before us a moment longer without speaking.

"Thank you," Sheila said, "you're very kind." She reached toward him and touched his hand.

"Goodbye," he said, and turned to the door. It was hard for him to talk to us. The screen door slapped after him, as he hurried outside.

When we'd finished eating, we carried the bag with us back across the field toward the highway. As we got closer to the car, we saw that someone had covered it with freshly cut flowers. Minutes later the tow truck arrived, and we climbed into the cab with the driver. As the truck pulled onto the highway and came up to speed, my little car in tow, flowers streamed through the air behind us like the tail of a comet.

The truck pulled my car to a garage on the outskirts of Memphis and dropped it gently on the lot out front. Half an hour later the mechanic there explained that the engine was completely destroyed. "Threw a rod," he said. He was staring at Sheila as he talked, which wasn't doing his concentration much good. "The part that connects the crank to the piston," he tried. His face began to overheat. "Well, anyhow, the engine's shot on account of the damage to the block, crank and head." When Sheila smiled at him, the mechanic offered me a thousand dollars for the car. "That's the best I can do," he mumbled, looking down at his shoes. Even I knew that it was more than the car was worth.

"There's some camping stuff in the trunk," I told him. "Maybe you can get something for that, too."

He touched the bill of his cap. "Yes, Ma'am."

After I'd signed the papers for the car, the mechanic took us downtown in his truck. We crossed a long metal bridge and rolled through part of the city. Finally, he pulled into a temporary parking space in front of the bus station. "Good luck, now," he told us, as he lifted our bags from the bed of the truck. I was opening the door on my side when he ran around the truck to take my elbow. As he helped me down, I felt him slip something into my jacket pocket. At the time I thought it must be a love note with his phone number, but it turned out to be a silver St. Christopher medallion on a chain.

An hour later we were on our way to Cincinnati, via Nashville, where we had to change buses. It was a long trip and I was numb from losing the car, so as soon as the sun slipped behind the horizon, I fell asleep. When we got to Cincinnati, Sheila shook me. She was standing above me when I opened my eyes. "We've got to change buses now," she said. I followed her through a maze of parked vehicles to another bus, and together we boarded. Sheila pulled me by my elbow to a seat near the back. "Slide in here," she said, "and go back to sleep. I'm going to see about our luggage and a snack." Then she kissed my forehead and each of my cheeks.

When I woke again it was morning and Sheila was nowhere to be found. I walked up and down the aisle of the bus, tried the bathroom, and asked the driver, but her name was missing from the passenger list. The bus, I learned, was headed west.

In the pocket of my coat I found a ticket for Bakersfield and a big wad of cash, which I later counted in the bathroom: Five thousand, four hundred and sixty-three dollars. She'd given me all of it. For a long time I thought about getting off at the next stop and heading back to Ohio to look for her, but I knew it was useless. Somehow I was certain I'd never see Sheila again. Though I missed her, I wasn't sad. I knew that everything was turning out just the way it was meant to be. So I held my hands against my belly and closed my eyes as the bus rolled west. I ate sandwiches, looked out the window, read magazines, and slept in my seat until we reached Denver, where I found a room in a hotel near the terminal. The next day I walked back to the station, boarded another "scenic cruiser," and continued home.

My last night on the bus a man left his seat and moved down the aisle toward me. Though he looked away when I met his gaze, he licked his lips and slid into the empty seat beside me and started talking. I tried to ignore him, but he kept asking me questions and making me more and more uncomfortable with his talk. Finally he told me how beautiful I was, how excited I made him. "There's something about your skin that makes me want to touch it," he whispered. "You're so full of life."

His hand was twitching on his knee and I was wondering just what I'd do if it rose up and reached for me, when a tall, exotic-looking woman with dark skin and eyes and long, thick hair exited the restroom at the back of the bus and moved up the aisle. When she stopped next to us and stood above the man, I saw she was wearing a gold ring in her nose. "I'm afraid you've taken my seat while I was in the restroom," she said. She spoke with a slight British accent.

I could feel the man beside me twitch and hesitate. "There wasn't anyone sitting here," he finally said.

The woman leaned down close to his face. "You've got my seat," she growled, her voice low, her eyes burning brightly. The man stiffened as she stared him down. Then he excused himself, stood, and walked up the aisle. The woman watched him move away, then slid into the vacant seat beside me. "I'm Monique," she said, extending a cool, dry hand. Almost immediately, she closed her eyes and dropped off to sleep. I could hear her breathing next to me. When she awoke an hour or so later, she stretched her arms high above her head so that her halter blouse rose up, revealing the top inch of a thick white ridge of scar along her belly. I closed my eyes and slept. When I woke she was gone.

It was noon when the bus pulled into Bakersfield. For a moment it felt good to be home again, and I wondered if I ought to take a taxi to the restaurant and see if I could get my old job back. But I figured there would be plenty of time for that later, after I'd cleaned up and rested from the trip. So I put my suitcase into a key-operated luggage locker in the station and sat down to enjoy a snack from the lunch counter nearby. I'd never been so hungry. After I'd finished eating, I hired a taxi to drive me home. "Been gone long?" the driver asked, trying to make conversation.

"Not really," I said. Suddenly everything around me began to look depressingly familiar. I thought of the truckers, the bowling alleys, the country music bars. "Turn around," I said to the driver.

"What?" He looked at me as if he hadn't quite heard me.

"Nothing," I said. "I'm kind of turned around, is all. I've been gone a long time." He shrugged his shoulders and rolled his eyes slightly. "Longer than I thought, before, I guess."

When I got to the trailer park, the manager there handed me an overnight delivery package. "This came for you just this morning," he said. "I told the driver you'd been out of town for months and I didn't know when you were coming back, but he said his instructions were to leave it and to come back in a week for it if you hadn't claimed it by then." There was no return address on the envelope. I took the packet back to my trailer, sat down on the stoop, and ripped it open with the serrated edge of my house key.

Inside was a photostat of a birth certificate embossed with the seal of the state of Ohio. From this document I learned that a brown-haired, brown-eyed female, weighing seven and a half pounds, had been born on Christmas day, thirty years earlier. The mother was listed as Mary McKenzie, aged fourteen, the father unknown. The child had been named after the mother by the resident social worker. In a box on the top left corner of the page was a handwritten note stating that the child had been legally adopted three weeks after birth, on what I'd always celebrated as my birthday, by my parents, Mr. and Mrs. Harold R. Kingsley. Penciled across the bottom of the paper were the words GOD IS LOVE.

I'm not sure exactly what happened next. I know from what I've been told that my neighbors found me wandering around the trailer park without any clothes on. I was clutching a tiny dashboard statuette of the Virgin Mary, and I didn't know who I was. It was clear that I'd suffered some kind of shock and couldn't take care of myself, but I'm better now.

Even so, after all I've been through, I can't say with certainty whether or not I really saw a halo of white birds hover around Sheila's head as she stood near the church in New Orleans, nor whether she strangled with her bare hands a rattlesnake that had crawled into my bed one night in our hotel room in Albuquerque, nor whether Chiquita's motorcycle left the road and drifted skyward as she departed. I don't know for sure that flowers bloomed out of season everywhere we went or that Sheila sometimes had a tattoo of a rose on her breast. I can't prove that she healed with her touch a dog that had been hit by a car along the highway or whispered to a deaf man in the bus station and made him laugh. At this point I'm not even sure about the angels I saw jump from the overpass in Bakersfield.

All that's really important now is that my baby is due any day. The doctors have told me what I already knew, that you are a girl. If I have struggled these past weeks to record this sequence of events, it is only because I want you to know why you have been named after Sheila.